THE SHAPE
OF THE EARTH

Praise for *Young and In Love?*

By the Author

The Man Who Asked to Be Killed
(A Few Good Books Publishing, 2014)

Young and in Love?

The Shape of the Earth

Visit us at www.boldstrokesbooks.com

THE SHAPE
OF THE EARTH

by

Gary Garth McCann

2019

THE SHAPE OF THE EARTH

ISBN 13: 978-1-63555-391-8

This Trade Paperback Original Is Published By
Bold Strokes Books, Inc.
P.O. Box 249
Valley Falls, NY 12185

First Edition: March 2019

CREDITS
Editor: Jerry L. Wheeler
Production Design: Stacia Seaman
Cover Design by Melody Pond

Acknowledgments

A version of part of Chapter One appeared as the story "The Shape of the Earth" in *The Q Review* (2011), reprinted in *Off the Rocks*, vol. 16 (Chicago: New Town Writers, 2012).

A version of part of Chapter Two appeared as the story "The Best I Can Do Under the Circumstances" in *Best Gay Love Stories 2005* (Nick Street, ed., Los Angeles: Alyson Books).

For this book and for *Young and in Love?* I'm indebted to editor Jerry L. Wheeler for helping me toward my goal of writing fiction that readers will never be tempted to skim.

For my husband, Todd

1. THE DANGER OF BUYING UNDERWEAR

Dave comes out of his den when he hears me in the kitchen. We kiss, and I ask about his overnight trip to Fresno. His panel went well, he says. "Five people in the audience, but I'll get a paper out of it." He's up for tenure next year.

As we eat, I tell Dave about helping a new guy at work— Ian—carry his drunk, obese mother to bed after I gave him a ride home because his car wouldn't start. I'm nervous. I hired Ian in August, and it's January. I've kept Ian a secret because my fantasies about him are so sexy. Maybe I'll say I hired him in November, if Dave asks. Or maybe I'll say Jane hired him, and I'll go off on a rant about how hiring is supposed to be my job.

Dave doesn't ask.

After we clean up, I sit on the living room floor and listen to sitar music through headphones while staring at a candle. I once thought you had to smoke a joint to be mesmerized by a flame.

Taking off my headphones, I slip to the doorway of Dave's den. The room is warm from the ceiling light and the high-intensity desk lamp. Stripped to his navy-colored briefs, he leans over his laptop. He's working on another paper he hopes to get published. I want to kiss his muscular neck or ruffle his brown hair, boyishly full at thirty-two. Instead, I tiptoe back to my music and candle.

When I go to look at Dave again, his den is empty. Seeing light in our bedroom, I lean in through the doorway. He lies on his back atop the green comforter on our high double bed, our only antique. He drapes his forearm over his eyes. His square jaw is clenched.

"You look worried, cowboy."

As though he doesn't hear me, he remains still—large unmoving feet, long still legs, tensed torso, his hand behind his neck contracting his biceps into a bulge. He bites his lip.

"Do you want a cup of tea or something?" I say.

Lifting his arm from his face, he raises his legs and pulls off his underwear in a backward S motion and pitches it against the closet door. Like a dog on its back, he displays his egg-sized testicles while his penis sleeps on his belly. I watch it come to life and bounce against his midriff.

"I want you to come here and fuck me, Lenny."

I am Man. I could beat my chest and roar it. I'm Tarzan, Superman. I'm the naked Olympic fighter with fists raised as I and my opponent step into the ancient earthen ring. We fight with full erections, and the crowd cheers and hungers to see who will have an erection when we finish, which swordsman will still have a sword. I feel it all in my dick, feel every manly thing the word embodies. I am man *enough.* I am so much man, my manhood hurts with exquisite pain.

We lie kissing afterward. Each whispers more than once that he loves the other. I'm a normal human being again, back from my foray into super manliness. Just me here, folks, Lenny—the guy who'd sooner run than fight.

Dave gets up and crosses the hall to the bathroom. He pisses and pads into his den to work more. I lie listening to the late Thursday evening traffic rush past our house. Living on a busy street isn't bad. We're not enmeshed in neighborliness, as we might be otherwise. We exist in a private world, a world that couldn't be more perfect.

❖

Ian grins at Rosie and chews coconut cream pie with his mouth as wide open as he can without spewing it all over. We stand behind the bookstore's service counter, Ian's neat white teeth glistening with saliva and looking handsome to me despite the glob of cream, custard, and crust.

Rosie laughs and makes a face. "*Que puerco!*" Ian thrusts out his pie-covered tongue, curving its tip to the cleft in his chin. Rosie rolls her caramel-colored eyes to the ceiling. "*Gross*, Ian! Such a child!"

Ian glances at me from between dark lashes. He looks away, silhouetting the ragged edge of his coal-black bangs. "Lenny doesn't think it's gross," he says.

I'm surprised by his flirting but figure he's playing the straight guy who knows the gay guy's attracted to him. Ian's in the homophobic stage some guys go through before coming out. I have such a mental hard-on for him, I'm willing to play along.

"Lenny's no *judge*," Rosie says. "Lenny thinks you're so hot, he'd eat out of your open mouth." Rosie puts her arm around my waist and body-bumps me. A junior at Cal State, she's large-boned and shapely, with light brown skin and auburn hair piled high in a loose bun. A friend of hers dated Ian and dropped him because he didn't screw her enough or didn't screw her *well* enough. Rosie became discreet when pressed for details.

I grin and slip my arm around her shoulders. "You're in a festive mood, Rosie."

She cackles. "Jane's daughter-in-law will kill her before their ship gets out of harbor."

Royal Books' proprietor, Jane, leaves tomorrow for a Caribbean cruise with Chip and his wife. Chip's the younger of Jane's two USC-lawyer sons, the one my age, a fact Jane loves to remind me of when she tells me about the rich and successful things her sons are doing. I could do rich and successful things if I inherited a small fortune from my grandparents.

I glance at Jane to make sure she didn't overhear Rosie's remark. Blonder than I, Jane wears a yellow Shetland sweater with yellow skirt and heels. She never wears the same outfit twice, never the same shoes. A small country could eat on the money Jane spends for clothes. She fingers a pearl choker around her scrawny neck as she bends the ear of a greeting card salesman eating pie with us, pie I brought to celebrate Ian's twenty-fifth birthday.

When everyone says they've had enough, I carry a tin with a third left to the refrigerator in the stockroom.

Just past three, I follow Ian's handsome butt, in gray khakis reaching deep into his crack, to the stockroom and through its swinging door. He takes his time card from the rack and punches out.

"Why don't we finish the pie before you go, Ian?"

I don't expect enthusiasm because Ian doesn't want to appear to *like* me. I open the refrigerator and take out the pie tin. With a plastic knife, I halve what's left and maneuver the slices onto paper plates. As we dig in, Ian leans against the wall with one knee raised, the sole of his black sneaker flat to the Sheetrock.

We watch each other eat. He opens his mouth, exposing a partially chewed mass. I smile and open my mouth, exposing the same. We chew with slow, exaggerated movement and swallow. Ian forks more pie. Slipping his fork into his mouth, he looks at me with purpose. I move closer, and we kiss, our tongues sliding into sweet globs of pie. I straddle his knee, pressing my erection against his raised leg. He shoves me backward. I expect to see someone at the stockroom door, but no one's there.

We stare at each other as we finish our pie.

I follow him out through the stockroom's swinging door as Rosie strides toward us with the grace of a big cat, under her arm an oversized gift book, a photograph of the Grand Canyon on its dust jacket. "Dave's on the phone for you, Lenny, and a woman wants to buy this but doesn't want the display copy. Do we have another one?"

"I'll check," Ian says, taking the book from her and turning around.

I follow Rosie behind the service counter, her hips swaying in a long, brown sweater that clings to her jeans. She stops by the cash register, and I continue into my office and pick up the phone. Dave calls me on Royal Books' number because Jane forbids staff to use cells.

"Dave."

"Sorry if I interrupted something," he says.

"You didn't interrupt anything."

"I forgot to mention Robert's having a party tonight. I figure we'll go?"

"Sure."

Robert heads the literature department at Cal State. He's like a doting gay uncle to Dave and me.

"How's your day going?" Dave says.

"Ordinary." I hear guilt in my voice, but Dave wouldn't. I listen to him blow off steam about the dean insisting he change a student's fall grade while my mind flits to being sued by Ian for sexual harassment. Through my office window I watch Ian hand a copy of the Grand Canyon book to Rosie. Getting a boner, I turn from the window and gaze at my wall calendar, a snow scene of Yosemite on the page for January. The calendar was among Dave's Christmas gifts to me.

❖

Pixie-sized Robert spots us from across his living room. His vibrant gray eyes smile from baby-soft mottled skin as he makes his way around and between his chatting guests. "Hello, boys. Fashionably late, I see." His voice is playful, raspy. His hands dart out from the sleeves of a baggy maroon cardigan, landing on our forearms. He offers a cheek to be kissed. A shock of hair swings out from Dave's forehead as he leans to oblige Robert. I glance to see who I know among the middle-aged academics, the group nearest us moaning about recent political outrages. I'm startled to spot Ian in a circle of grad students across the room. Ian's working on an MA in comp lit. I know he took a class from Robert, but I've never seen him at Robert's house. On Ian's arm is a willowy brunette with hair down to the small of her back. She's dropped him off at the bookstore a time or two.

Ian doesn't see me. I look away, but his blue-black hair and long-sleeved red T-shirt glow in my peripheral vision. "What's the matter?" Dave says.

"Nothing." I kiss Robert's cheek.

"I'll put the beer we brought in the refrigerator."

I lean down to Robert's ear. "You know Ian Ryan?"

Robert laughs and plays at making insinuating eyes. "Melinda, my research assistant brought him. She has excellent taste, don't you think?"

"She does. Ian works for me."

Robert flicks his silver eyebrows. "Small world. Lucky you."

Ian sees me, turns his back, and slips his arm around Melinda's waist. Her sleeveless mint dress looks suitable for a wedding, as though this casual party means more to her than it should. I like her for the needy life that suggests. I figure when Dave returns, I'll introduce him to Ian and get my nervous moment over. Dave will razz me about hiring a guy as hot as Ian, and my Ian fantasies won't feel like imaginable realities anymore because Ian won't be a secret. Good.

Robert pats my forearm and excuses himself to say a word to a couple leaving. I turn and head to Dave, talking to our friend Sandy by the long dining table.

"Hi, sweetie," I shout over the music as someone cranks up the volume in the family room. Sandy and I peck on the lips. "You're looking good," I tell her. She's short and always fighting weight, her red hair stylishly boyish and framing a pretty face with a clear complexion. As I bend down to listen to her, my back to the living room, Melinda passes from behind me, leading Ian by the hand. They stop at the far end of the table. While Melinda greets two women grad students, Ian picks up a vodka bottle and fills a tumbler more than halfway. I wink when he looks up. He nods hello, just barely, and pours orange juice into his vodka.

Sandy tugs my hand while I'm staring at Ian. "Let's go out back so I can smoke."

She leads me through the family room, between dancing couples who look too settled in life, too love-handled for partying hard. Outside, beyond a sliding glass door, the smokers spill from the patio onto the small lawn, made even smaller by dripping bamboo towering on three sides. Sandy and I stop near a round stone table, damp from fog, at the edge of light cast by the house.

A joint comes our way, and I decide one hit won't hurt. Holding smoke in my lungs, I stare through the glass door as

Melinda and Ian join the dancers in the family room. I let out smoke. "You must know Ian Ryan?" I ask Sandy. She's the literature department secretary.

"I know Melinda better."

"You don't like Melinda?"

"She's all right—a little headstrong." Frowning, Sandy draws on her cigarette and exhales through small nostrils. "I wouldn't do Ian any favors, babe."

"What have you got against Ian? I like him."

Sandy twists her mouth. "Speaking of people I don't like, how's Jane?"

"Away on a cruise, hallelujah!"

Sandy worked at Royal Books when I started there; Jane loved to hate her.

"You're a patient man, Lenny. I owe you big-time for hooking me up with Robert. He's a dream of a boss."

"So, why don't you like Ian?"

Sandy shakes her head and stubs out her cigarette in a wet ashtray on the table. She looks around at the other smokers and crosses her arms with a shiver. I wear a sweater, but she's in a sleeveless blouse. I place my arm around her shoulders. "You're cold, sweetie. Let's go dance."

I maneuver us near Ian and Melinda, among the crowd bumping and grinding. Sandy looks more distressed than happy. She needs a boyfriend, I figure. A son in college and a friendly ex-husband aren't enough. I reach out and brush my fingertips along her cheeks, and she brightens.

Robert joins us as one song blends into another. I pull my sweater over my head and toss it among shed layers on a couch shoved against a wall. Robert's eyes flit to my gray muscle shirt. In his cups on my last birthday, my thirtieth, he told me he likes thirty-year-old blonds.

"I'm not into dancing tonight," Sandy shouts. She air-kisses Robert and me and scoots away.

As a new song begins, I face Robert while Melinda, beside me, faces Ian. Judging by Ian's glazed-over eyes, he chugged all the vodka he poured. He raises his arms on an upbeat lyric, and I mentally trace the contours of his compact torso as his shirt rides above a navel that looks like an etching on his flat stomach.

"People are leaving, and I want to say good night," Robert shouts to Melinda. "You and Ian dance with Lenny."

I turn halfway to Melinda. She smiles until Robert disappears, then gives me a look that says she knows I'm admiring her date and doesn't appreciate it. Fair enough, I think. "I need a beer."

Slipping between the dancers, I find my sweater on the couch and toss it over my shoulder. I wonder where Dave is.

He's not in the living room. From the hallway, I glance into Robert's den and see Dave sitting forward on a black leather sofa, his back to me, his large hands raised in a shrugging gesture. He's talking to an engineering professor named Brian, a young Paul Newman. Dave's in the biology department but knows Brian from playing city-league baseball. Brian's pregnant wife, a lawyer, is with them. I watch Dave sitting erect in a white pullover sweater, his long spine straight, his angular face relaxed and smiling in half profile. He doesn't know I'm watching him and thinking I made a good decision when I moved to California to be with him. If I'd asked myself whether I was in love in the beginning, I didn't ask for long.

I glance at Brian and wonder if Dave's attracted to him. I'm sure Dave gets a hard-on for as many guys as I do. He won't admit it. He's afraid of encouraging me. He thinks I don't have his willpower. We're not ready for a big wedding yet, but we wear rings, Dave's idea to help keep me in line.

I head for the kitchen, a pale green room with dark cabinets and a butcher block island laden with booze and soft drinks, platters of broccoli and cheese glistening and looking plastic under ceiling spotlights. I take a bottle of beer from a cooler on the floor, lean back against the counter, and savor being alone in relative quiet. Ian appears in the doorway, stops when he sees me, and then takes a few unsteady steps to the island, where he picks up a Pepsi.

"Did you down all the vodka you poured, Ian?"

Without answering, he leans against the stove at a right angle to me. His tanned, square-tipped fingers fumble until he snaps the can open and mist rises.

"Where's the lady you're with?" I say.

"In the john." He gulps, his Adam's apple bobbing. He flexes the can's thin metal. "You should give me Jack's hours, Lenny."

Jack, the bookstore's evening manager, is quitting. Mai-Ly, who has seniority over Ian, asked for Jack's hours. Ian knows I told her she could have them.

"You're drunk, Ian. Why would you want Jack's hours?"

"So you and I won't be working at the same time."

"What? Like I'm the only man you've ever been attracted to?"

"You don't know what you're talking about, Lenny."

Melinda comes into the kitchen, and I take a swallow of beer. "Your date's had too much to drink."

"Oh, yes." Melinda shakes her head, tch-tching, and slips an arm around his waist. She steers him from the room.

I finish my beer in no hurry, lift my sweater off my shoulder, and pull it on.

Dave still sits in the den with Brian. Brian's wife isn't with them. They're talking about who will win the Super Bowl, but I couldn't care less. Dave glances at me as I sit down beside him. He looks back at Brian and keeps talking but holds a hand my way. I take it, lean back, and map the bones in my cowboy's fingers while he talks to Brian.

Yawning, Dave asks if I'm ready to go.

"Whenever you are."

"I should find my wife," Brian says, rising to his feet. We follow him out of the den.

Melinda and Ian sit on the living room sofa, Melinda talking to one of the grad students she greeted earlier. Ian slouches down on the cushions, an ankle crossed over a knee, his head tipped back against the top of the couch. He catches sight of Dave and me and, without lifting his head, rotates it to follow us as we pass. I look over my shoulder from the front door and meet his gaze.

❖

In Jane's driveway, in the hills above downtown Fullerton, Ian and I strain under the weight of a display table we unload from a van Ian rented on the store credit card. Ian is house-sitting while Jane cruises. We upend the table against the wall in her chilly garage. I wipe my face with the front of my sweatshirt. "We'll never use this goddamn table in the store again, but Jane can't throw anything away."

I follow Ian out to the sunny driveway, and he lowers the garage door, hiding Jane's Cadillac. Her white Spanish house sits above and to the side, on the highest point of a ridge. Newer houses—elegant ranchers—line the road as it descends in both directions from Jane's property.

Ian looks up at the cement steps curving to her front door through terraces shored up with wire mesh and planted with ivy and squat junipers. "Have you ever been inside?"

I shake my head. "I've heard enough about it. She has a conniption fit picking new shelf paper for her kitchen cabinets."

"The view's fantastic from the back. Do you want to see it?"

I follow him up the steps and in the front door. He leads me past a sand-colored living room with a wagon wheel coffee table and out French doors to a terrace. Santa Ana winds have blown away last night's fog, and the view at our feet encompasses much of North Orange County as it slopes to the ocean.

Ian glances to see if I'm impressed. I refuse to be effusive over anything connected to Jane.

"That's Catalina." He points at what appears to be a low, brown cloud on the silver horizon.

I realize he's right. "I can see why you like staying here."

"At night, with the lights spread out below, it feels like you're in an airplane."

I watch his eye follow a jet, far enough away to look toy like as it descends to Orange County Airport.

"I've only flown once in my life," he mumbles.

"Coming from Ireland?"

"Going to San Francisco. Well, twice, going and coming back. I've never been out of California, except as a baby."

"When did you go to San Francisco?"

"A couple of years ago. This girl I knew took me for my birthday. All she wanted to do was stay in our hotel room and have sex."

I laugh out loud. "Were you a disappointment to her, Ian?"

"I wanted to go out and at least see *something*."

Smiling, I glance down a sheer embankment planted

with trailing gazanias. A rectangular swimming pool nestles in a cut on the chaparral-covered hillside, silver green from recent rain. Dark blue tiles frame the pale blue body of water. Weathered redwood lounges with faded green cushions stretch like lizards at odd angles to one another around the white cement deck.

"Want to go for a swim?" Ian says.

I stare down a steep flight of railroad tie steps sunk into the cliff, with a round, rusty handrail on one side. In an arroyo a few hundred yards below the pool, the tops of eucalyptus trees mask the roofs of houses on a snaking road. "Sure, let's go for a swim."

We strip off our clothes at the bottom of the steps while the boom of a grasshopper oil derrick, just visible around the curve of the hillside, rises and falls above ragged olive trees. Ian's light tan body shows a bathing suit line fainter than mine. I watch his backside as he dives into the water, and then I follow. The pool is so full, ripples slosh onto the deck.

We swim laps leisurely. When he swims faster, I stay with him.

He quits and glides to the side, faces inward and watches me. I swim a few more laps before pulling up next to him. He turns and hugs the pool wall, his chest flush to it, gleaming arms folded in the sun on the dark blue tile edge, one hand over the other. I grip the lip and let my upright body sink till I'm submerged to my shoulders. The water undulates from our swimming, and my chest drifts to the wall and away.

"How'd you feel this morning, after all the vodka you drank last night?"

He doesn't answer. He lifts his arms off the tile edge and drops underwater to his neck.

I let my body drift closer to his. The wind chills my head, and my nose runs and stings from chlorine, all I can smell.

"Do you remember coming into the kitchen for a Pepsi and talking to me?"

We're shoulder to shoulder. I feel his toes caress the arch of my foot. He stretches toward me, and we kiss. I slip my hand under his buttocks, and he kisses me harder. I bend my middle finger into his crack and gently nudge his anus. His buttocks squeeze.

"Hello! Hello!" a woman shouts from above. "I'm here!"

We look up at Melinda.

"Be right there," Ian bellows, his voice deep.

Ian hoists himself out of the water. I watch his curved, bruise-colored erection as he walks around the pool to the side where our clothes are. Melinda's out of sight when I look up again. I climb onto the deck. Ian and I shiver in the wind, letting it dry us some as we shake droplets off our limbs. He kicks into jeans, grabs his T-shirt, sweater, socks, and shoes, and hustles up the railroad tie steps.

Letting the air dry me more, I gaze around the hillside in the low sun's gold light. A jackrabbit emerges from the brush, and we watch each other as I pull on my pants and sweatshirt. It scampers away. I pick up my old deck shoes and leisurely climb barefoot up the steps.

Melinda's in the kitchen. Her pink sweater, black jeans, and white tennis shoes remind of a three-tone '50s Dodge I saw at an antique car show. Her hair is pulled back in a knot, her face bare except for pink lipstick. I smell coffee and hear a shower running.

"Do you want some coffee? You must be freezing."

"Thanks."

She fills a large white mug with a bright yellow ring around its lip. Behind her, a curtain billows at one side of the window over the sink.

"Milk or sugar?"

"Black."

I take the mug and sit at the kitchen table of Shaker simplicity, thin wood top on broomstick legs that angled out. The kitchen is cream colored.

Melinda leans back against the counter. Her light blue eyes watch me as though I'm an experimental mouse about to exhibit an important reaction. I swallow a little coffee.

She raises her eyebrows. The sound of the shower stops, and she glances at another part of the house, then sips from her mug. She lowers it and pinches the bridge of her nose. "You wouldn't be here if..."

"I'm not your rival, Melinda."

"I'm not *your* rival."

"I'm in a relationship."

"*Are* you?"

A timer goes off, and she sets her coffee mug down to slide a casserole dish into the oven. "Ian and I are friends," she says, picking up her mug and leaning against the counter again. "I care what happens to him."

I watch her stare at the floor until Ian pads into the room in tan shorts and a black T-shirt, his head damp. I gulp the last of my coffee, wiggle my feet into my deck shoes, and rise from my chair. "Time for me to go. See you at work, Ian."

He follows me to the front door. I let myself out and hustle down the curving steps through the reinforced terraces. My hatchback sits by the rented van. Starting my engine, I pat my steering wheel as though my car were a faithful dog. Melinda arrived just in time. I'll keep plenty of distance between Ian and me, I decide driving home.

I'm only the second man Dave's had sex with in his life. I wasn't ready to settle down when we met, but I made the mistake of getting an apartment with him when we both lived in Washington, DC. He moved out after he caught me on the living room floor with our long-haired neighbor who looked like Jesus. We had dinner a few times over the next several months, and then he moved to take his job, ABD, at Cal State.

❖

Sitting on the washing machine, holding my phone after a Sunday afternoon talk with my mom in Galveston, I recall something she said before Dave and I were together.

"If you want to squeeze out of those jeans, Lenny, honey, I'll fix that stuck zipper. To tell the truth, I'd rather fix your other pants so they don't unzip so easily."

My mom's a tall, wiry woman with frizzy gray hair. She never wears much makeup. On the phone, she said it's cold in Texas, so she's probably wearing a sweater and slacks. She asked how her other son was. She loves Dave for making me settle down, among other reasons. I love Dave for making me settle down, among other reasons, too.

I put on shoes, grab my car keys, and drive across town, past Cal State. In a discount store, I buy underwear for Dave and me in navy blue, forest green, and burgundy. Dave's working in his office on campus and won't be home until suppertime.

It's dark outdoors when my car bumps up the driveway of a doughnut shop near the college. I want a cup of coffee. I pull into a parking space facing the plate glass of the bare-bones eating room. As I shut off my engine, I glance through the lighted windows. Ian sits in one of the pastel booths in the bright glare. He's leaning forward and grinning, holding a bent drinking straw, wrapping the straw around his index finger. Sitting across from Ian is Dave, also leaning forward and grinning, holding a crumpled paper coffee cup, crushing the cup with his fingertips. I watch them gaze at each other.

They rise from the booth, and I start my car. They walk to the door, laughing and talking, and I back out of my parking space. I roll quickly down the driveway and out.

At home, I pour a glass of red wine and take chicken breasts out of the refrigerator, coat them in olive oil, and season them for the grill. I take lettuce and tomatoes out of the crisper.

What could be keeping Dave? He and Ian ran into each other on campus, recognized each other from Robert's party, and went for a cup of coffee. Simple.

The sound of Dave's car idling in the alley behind our house tells me he's raising the garage door. Taking broccoli from the refrigerator, I pare off the stems and drop the florets into an old, tarnished steamer. The kitchen door opens and Dave appears, dressed in a gray pullover sweater, painter's pants, and blue running shoes, sockless. His battered, fat leather briefcase dangles at his side. He kisses me and looks at the chicken on the counter. "Good. I'm hungry."

"I'll start the grill, and we can eat early. How was your afternoon?"

"Okay."

He carries his briefcase into his den and goes into our bedroom, then returns to the kitchen with his sweater and shoes off, his white T-shirt webbed with gray fuzz.

"Did you get a lot of work done?" I say.

"I looked up some stuff in the library, finished a draft of my article. What'd you do this afternoon?"

"Read. Talked to my mom. Went to buy underwear. I'm making coffee. Do you want a cup?"

"I had coffee just before I left the office. Should I throw together a salad?"

"If you want to. Maybe I won't bother making coffee." A

small red ant crawls across the faded beige countertop, toward the toaster. I crush it with my index finger and rinse my hand under the tap. "Are you sure you don't want coffee, Dave?"

"Positive."

"Maybe I'll have more wine."

After refilling my wineglass, I set it and the plate of chicken breasts on a tray and flip on the outdoor light.

A pink block wall hides our backyard from the alley and from the backyards of our neighbors, a Vietnamese family who bought just before we did and an elderly widow from Missouri who moved in with her husband in the fifties, when the development was new. A jade tree hedge grows against the wall at the back of the yard, and at the side, against the garage, a bougainvillea. Dave and I planted a palm tree in the middle and birds-of-paradise and agapanthuses near the house.

I step barefoot along the cold, narrow walk from our kitchen door to the alley and stop by our three-legged barbecue grill, in moist grass near a wood gate through the block wall. I dump charcoal into the bowl, squirt on lighter fluid, and toss in a match. A ball of bright orange flame lights up the night air like a small sun. Staring into the flame, I tell myself things aren't always as they appear. The earth looks flat and doesn't feel like it's moving. I try to remember at what age I learned the earth is round and rotating.

We eat in front of the TV, and Dave works in his den until bedtime.

Did he avoid me at Robert's party? Did he and Ian avoid each other? Is that why Dave sat in Robert's den for most of the two hours we were there?

In bed, he's tired—not unheard of on a Sunday night. We had sex before we went to Robert's party Friday, and again Saturday morning and Saturday night. We kiss, and Dave falls asleep. I fall asleep eventually, an uneasy sleep fret with dreams.

I wake gasping, soaked in sweat. After shoving down my half of the covers, I take deep breaths until my heart stops racing. In a slow motion nightmare, with air as dark and sticky as molasses, I drove head-on toward another car with Melinda at its wheel. Sandy was in the car with Melinda, and they were both silently screaming at me.

2. YOU DESERVE BETTER

Gray light seeps around the closed curtain. The radio will come on in two minutes. Dave sleeps facing me, his knees raised, taking more than half the bed. I see his thick head of hair more than his face burrowed into his pillow. Pulling with me my edge of the sheet and blanket, I scoot down, askew to Dave's zigzagging body. My feet stick off the mattress near the foot. Watching his twitching erection point at my waiting mouth, I wonder whether he's dreaming. Our radio comes on, a female pop singer.

I nose beside Dave's cock and stick my tongue into his navel, as textured as a halved walnut husk with the meat removed. I slide my tongue down the fuzz below his belly button and lick my way out the length of his shaft. I wrap my lips around his head. He gently pushes in and pulls out. His big toe caresses my calf, his fingertips churn my hair. His thrusts become more intense but remain smooth, controlled, never violent.

"I'm gonna give you my love, Lenny," he breathes softly. In and out, in again. "Here it comes, Len. I love you." Once, twice, three times. His semen tastes like bread dough. Craving it like air, I'm glad I'll go to work with it in my stomach. His bone softens to a fulsome penis, the archetype of every husky wiener I've glimpsed since boyhood. I love it as much this way and keep it in my mouth until I come.

Dave pulls me up, and we kiss. The radio plays ads. A second song hasn't started yet. Sex is so simple between two men.

❖

I wait for Ian with a taste for blood in my mouth. Mai-Ly clocks in at ten, when Ian's due, and walks behind the counter. Mai-Ly is petite, in a powder-blue dress and a small white unbuttoned sweater, her long, straight black hair parted in the middle, framing her delicate features. Mai-Ly's ex-boyfriend taught her about honesty in bed, she told me. After their breakup, she said he'd told her he couldn't go to bed with her anymore because he sometimes thought of other women. I listened and considered the moments my roving mind flashed on other men when I'm in bed with Dave. Mai-Ly took comfort in her boyfriend's rationale for breaking up with her, so I didn't tell her there wouldn't be any long-term relationships if everyone was as strict as her boyfriend about where his mind wandered in bed.

"Ian had to take his mother to the hospital," Mai-Ly says.

"The hospital?"

"Not an emergency—some procedure."

I pat the oak veneer counter a few times, as though I'm a bongo drummer. "Don't you have a class now, Mai-Ly?"

"I told him I could miss this once."

"Don't let him bully you."

"He wouldn't."

"Don't be so sure."

Mai-Ly settles on the stool by the register. Drumming the

counter a few more times, I think of what I'm going to say to the son of a bitch when he gets here.

From the stockroom I carry an empty box to a revolving rack of wall calendars and begin pulling them. Opening a dog-eared display copy of a baseball calendar, I leaf through a few glossy pages and stop at a picture of a batter leaning over home plate. In a drawer at home are pictures of Dave as a shortstop for Georgetown and for the Wisconsin Rapids Twins. Near the end of his first Twins season, he made the mistake of thinking a mutual spark existed between him and his best friend on the team. In his second season, his teammates kept him at a polite distance, and his so-so playing suffered. Before the season ended, he left to start grad school, an option he'd kept open.

I stare at the ballplayer in the calendar, a man attractive enough to keep me from flipping to the next month. He could be anyone, for my knowledge of baseball. All I know about him is that I'd like to see him come, to experience his body at its peak. However many men I've had, I want more. No one expects less of a straight man in his craving for women, do they?

Near noon, Ian breezes through the bookstore's clean glass doors in a black T-shirt, bone-colored pants, and flip-flops. He carries a small doughnut sack and a worn paperback. From my office, I watch him disappear into the stockroom and wait a minute before following.

He sits on three stacked boxes and eats a jelly doughnut, straddling the corner of the top box, feet dangling, flip-flops hanging away from his heels. Virginia Woolf's *Jacob's Room* lies tucked under the curve of a buttock. He's read most of Woolf; we've talked a lot about her.

I lean against the wall, facing him. "How's your mom, Ian?"

"In good shape for the shape she's in. Everything's wrong with her."

"I'm sorry."

Shrugging, he pulls another doughnut out of the sack and bites into it. Red syrup oozes onto his fingers, and he licks them.

"I enjoyed the pool Saturday," I tell him. He fixes his dark blue eyes on the doughnut. I glance at the work schedule posted beside the bathroom door, to the right of his head. "Do you have plans for Friday night?"

"Do you want me to stay and close up?"

"I want you to come to our house for dinner, with Dave and me."

Ian wads up his doughnut sack. "Sorry. I'm tied up Friday night, come to think of it."

"Saturday night?"

"This week's bad. I'm trying to finish my Dostoevsky paper. The next few weeks are bad. Thanks, though, Lenny. I should clock in and get out there."

He hops off the boxes, tosses his wadded sack in a small plastic trash can, and turns to the time clock. I glance at the door to see if anyone's coming, move behind him, and curl my hands around his biceps. "You like me, and I like you. I know you'll like Dave, and he'll like you. I don't see a problem."

"Let go of me, Lenny."

I squeeze his muscles and let go. He punches in, and I follow him from the stockroom to the counter.

I watch through the interior window of my office while he takes over the register for Mai-Ly. She heads across the store and outdoors carrying a small can of tuna and an orange.

I mosey out to the counter and hoist myself up onto it, sit more or less facing Ian on his stool by the register, *Jacob's Room* open on his lap.

"What'd you do the rest of the weekend, Ian?"

"Nothing much."

"Nothing? Everybody does something."

"Worked on my Dostoevsky paper."

"In the library?"

"Some."

He looks up from his book, stares across the store, and cracks his knuckles. "This paper's turning out to be as long as my thesis."

"Is the campus fairly empty on weekends?"

"Fairly."

"Dave works in his office a lot of weekend afternoons."

Watching Ian stare ahead of himself, I give him a chance to say he ran into Dave in the library, recognized him from the party, and they went for coffee at a doughnut shop.

He cracks his knuckles again.

From my counter perch, facing my office, I look over my shoulder, in the direction he's staring. There's one customer in the store, a woman browsing the self-help medical section. "You seem nervous, Ian."

"I'm not nervous."

"Did anyone introduce you to Dave at Robert's party? I meant to."

He shakes his head and rises off his stool. "That woman's having trouble finding something. I'll go help her."

"You do that. I'll wait right here for you."

He hustles around the counter. I hop to the floor, turn, and watch him walk to the medical section. He talks to the woman and brings her to the service counter, where he searches our online inventory. In my office, I swivel my chair so my back's to him and try to concentrate on invoices I need to send to the bookkeeper. But I'm too pissed to do anything but leave for the gym.

When I come back after a long workout, Rosie stocks magazines near the door, her orange-lipsticked mouth open in a cavernous yawn. Ian's at the register. "Bored, Rosie?"

"Not enough sleep. This guy I'm seeing is an insomniac. He smokes joints and marches around the apartment imitating Mussolini."

"*Mussolini?* Lose him."

"He's doing a master's thesis on Mussolini, *querido*. And Alan's good in bed."

"Oh, well, if he's good in bed…"

She cackles. "We'll forgive a man his insane delusions if he's good in bed, eh, *querido*?"

"Damn right." I wink.

Heading to my office, carrying a sub to eat at my desk, I stop on the customer's side of the counter, across from Ian on his stool. He looks up from his book, and I lower my gaze to his smooth black T-shirt.

"I like seeing the points of your nipples in that shirt, Ian."

"Lenny, back off."

"Why?"

"Because I'm telling you to."

"*I know you're fucking Dave.*"

He stares past me, out the windows to the parking lot. "I don't know what you're talking about."

"I saw you guys having coffee in the doughnut shop near the college."

"So, I ran into a guy at a doughnut shop and had a cup of coffee with him."

"Bullshit. You're a lying bastard."

"Here comes a customer, Lenny." He hops off his stool. "I'll ring those up for you, ma'am."

I walk around the counter into my office and grab my

old leather jacket from the door hook. With it slung over my shoulder, I wait behind Ian while he finishes ringing up books. The woman pays and leaves. I glare at Ian. "I'm giving myself a few hours off. I deserve it, don't you think?"

"Sure, why not?"

He climbs on his stool and picks up *Jacob's Room*. He sits erect, staring ahead. I keep my eyes fixed on him until he glances at me and shrugs. "I won't tell Jane you left early. I never tell her anything."

"You can tell her whatever you want, bastard."

I hustle out of the store, climb into my car, and slam the door.

At home I open a bottle of beer. It's seventy-five degrees outside, and the late afternoon sun shines into the back of our small house. I'm used to getting home in the dark. After stripping off my shirt and shoes, I carry my beer out to the patio. With the sun on my shoulders, I pull weeds out from around our birds-of-paradise and agapanthuses.

Opening cans of corned beef hash for supper, I'm so absorbed in thinking about Dave with Ian I don't hear his car. He startles me when he comes in our back door. Salad is ready. We eat on the guestroom sofa watching the news and carry our dirty plates to the dishwasher.

"I need to finish writing the test I'm giving in 202 tomorrow. Do you want coffee, Len?"

"No, thanks."

Dave fills the teakettle and crosses to the stove. I lean against the counter and watch his lats stretch his T-shirt as he reaches for a coffee jar on a top shelf. He drinks instant when making coffee just for himself.

"I know you're fucking Ian, Dave."

He looks sideways at me, his mouth open.

"I thought I should tell you I know. I don't want to talk about it."

He turns his large body my way and freezes, like a big buck caught in the headlights of an oncoming car. I slip out of the room.

I start a cassette of Renaissance music in the living room. With headphones over my ears, I sit on the wood floor with my legs folded and stare into the fireplace as though the artificial log is blazing.

Dave comes out of the kitchen. He sits on the floor beside me and puts his arm around my shoulders. I consider knocking it off. He lifts the headphones away from my ears and holds them on his lap.

"I didn't know who he was, Len. You'd never mentioned a guy named Ian. He didn't know who I was. He thought I had a wife. We saw each other jogging and in the weight room."

"I said I don't want to talk about it."

"What do you want me to do? Can you give me a little time?"

"I can give you the rest of my life. Go write your test."

I take the headphones from him and put them over my ears. He kisses the back of my neck. I let him kiss me on the mouth—maybe then he'll go away and leave me alone. And he does.

In bed, I'm surprised when I can't stop kissing him. I pull him on top of me and raise my legs, wrap them around him. When I think of Ian doing the same thing, my erection throbs so hard it aches. "Fuck me, Dave," I breathe.

He rises on his knees on the bed, his back erect. He gets KY from the nightstand. "I want to kiss your balls first," I whisper. Despite myself, I crave showing him my respect for his manhood. He could have all the guys he wants but chose me, and he's tried to be faithful.

Dave stares into my eyes as he straddles me, inching his way to my head. He eases a large testicle into my mouth and watches me suck on it. I know that even with his pangs of guilt he feels cockier than ever right now, because he's having his way with two guys. Two of us are blowing him and raising our legs for him. I tell myself to let him savor his manhood. I savor it. Why shouldn't he?

He pulls his testicle out of my mouth and inserts the other one. While I squeeze it between my lips and watch his chest swell, he dabs KY on his head and presses my hand to it, to spread the gel along his shaft. He kisses me and hooks my ankles over his shoulders. I take him easily, despite his size. "Fuck me, lover," I whisper. I imagine Dave hearing Ian whisper the same words. I picture Ian below him.

"I love you, Len. With all my heart, I do." He comes and collapses on me. I stroke the back of his neck as he cries.

"I'd break it off right now if I could, Len," he says when he can talk. "Can you understand that?"

"Understanding doesn't mean I like it."

"I'm the only man Ian's ever had sex with. We haven't done anything unsafe, but you and I can go on a prescription if you think we should."

"Not as long as you use condoms."

"If you want me to move out for a while, I will."

"*No.* I don't want you to move out. You're infatuated, Dave. It'll pass. I'm pissed off. That'll pass, too."

"Can you handle this for a time?"

"Do I have a choice?"

He doesn't answer.

"I fucked around when we were first together. You're fucking around now. Our timing's off, but we're good together."

❖

At work over the next two weeks, Ian and I pretend to ignore each other. At home, Dave and I pretend Ian doesn't exist.

❖

Locked in the bathroom on Saturday night, I use a flashlight and a magnifying mirror to exam the inside of my mouth for sores, not that I'm aware of any. My gums are exemplary, no bleeding. A hygienist's poster boy, me. If I'm going to suck off someone other than Dave tonight, my mouth needs to be safe. I'll want the guy's cream.

In a gay dance bar, I taste my first hard liquor in five years—this after downing two beers, my normal limit. Dave comes out of the head and sees me with a rocks glass in my hand.

"What are you doing, Len?"

"Minding my own business, which is better than what some people are doing."

Earlier we met Robert for dinner at a coffee shop not far from the university. I talked to Robert and ignored Dave while we ate. When we left the restaurant, I got into Robert's car and let Dave drive alone. I'd swallowed my bile well enough until four days ago, Valentine's Day, when silent fury overcame me at the thought of Dave serving double duty.

I down my bourbon and signal the bartender for another. Someone tugs on my T-shirt, tucked through my jeans belt loop. "I *must* feel that sweaty torso," JT says in my ear. Small and effeminate, JT brings out the alpha dog in me, like Michael, my high school lover, did. All through senior year, I fucked small Michael, with his long, dark hair down his back. JT moves in front of me and presses the heels of his hands to my rib cage. He fans his fingers out across my pecs, avoiding my nipples. I'd like to squeeze the small waist under his purple shirt, bury my face in the long, brown hair beneath his bandana.

JT's shy lover, Billy, stares at the floor. A crew cut, tattooed albino, skinny in an oversized gray T-shirt and fatigues, Billy has the bass voice of a bullfrog and an uncut dick as big, limp, as a good-sized cucumber. At a Halloween party, Billy and I, both dressed as vampires, ducked into a closet and snuck a kiss.

Moving from me to Dave, JT splays his fingers around Dave's large nipples. Dave likes the flattery but doesn't have my eclectic taste in men. I give Billy a chesty hug. We both start to get hard and back off.

Turning to the bar, I pay for my double bourbon while JT and Billy take turns shouting in Robert's ear over the music.

Dave moves beside me. "Just don't drink too much, Lenny."

A late thirtyish man I noticed earlier walks to the men's room, brushing back his shaggy black hair, his hirsute olive-skinned chest thrust out. He sees me watching him, and he's curious.

I down my bourbon and follow him through the john's propped-open door. Stepping up next to him at the trough urinal, I watch him pee. He has a stout dick with a plum-sized head. "You have a nice bulbous cock," I say, affecting my Texas accent, as he tucks his plum through the fly of his jeans. He laughs. Piss streams from my gracefully arched member, which I hold between thumb and index finger. "My name's Lenny."

"Mine's Cleve."

"If I keep flirting with you, Cleve, I'll get a boner."

A couple of guys snicker. "No boners at the urinal," one of them says, in a mothering tone. Smiling, I shake dry and turn from the trough. I'm starting to get erect, so I make sure Cleve gets a glimpse before tucking myself away. We rinse our hands at the sinks and exit through the open door. "Let's dance," I shout.

I take his hand and lead him onto the floor, smile and ogle his chest, turn around and wiggle my butt. He's restrained, not much of a dancer.

After a few numbers, we move to the bar, where he orders a light beer and I my third double bourbon. Dave appears on my side opposite Cleve and shouts in my ear while he pulls on a green T-shirt with a coiled snake on its front, a souvenir he bought at the Cincinnati Zoo when we visited his folks last summer. "Robert's gone to JT and Billy's for coffee. I said we'd be along."

"Go ahead."

JT and Billy have a house twenty minutes away. I glance into my drink and swallow what's left.

"We don't have to go if you don't want to, Len."

"Go. I'm getting my own ride home."

"You're drinking too much."

"Fuck off, Dave."

I turn to Cleve. Staring at men dancing, he leans against the bar. Dave moves a couple of steps and resumes shouting in my ear. "Don't do anything crazy tonight. If you have to do something, make it safe."

I watch two shirtless, sweaty guys walk off the dance floor holding hands.

"Promise me, Len."

"*Christ!*"

"I love you. Nothing's changed about that."

I lean close to Dave's ear. "I won't do anything unsafe! Go home. I'll get there."

"If you're sure you want me to leave without you, I will."

"I'm sure."

"Should I get your jacket from the car?"

"*Go*, goddamn it!"

I face the bar, my back to Dave. He kisses me on the cheek. His mouth hovers near mine until I turn and kiss him. "Now go."

He backs away, does an about-face, and walks to the door, his tall body swaying in its unself-conscious gait.

I glance at Cleve, looking up to a suspended screen showing two men feeling each other's nipples. "You guys are married?"

"I don't know what we are."

"You wear wedding rings."

"You're going to take me home and feed me cock anyhow, aren't you?"

"If that's what you want."

"That's what I want. Let's have a nightcap and get out of here."

I order my bourbon neat. Cleve orders a Coke.

We down our drinks and wander bare chested out into the well-lit, cold parking lot. I pull my T-shirt out of my belt loop and slip it on. Cleve unlocks the passenger side of a big metallic green American sedan and picks up a silver bomber jacket from the front seat. As I slide into the car, I watch his hairy arms and chest disappear into the jacket.

We float down the Costa Mesa Freeway with a fluid motion that reminds me of lying on a raft in a gently undulating pool. The new car smell and the blowing heater make my stomach queasy.

"You have a big-ass new car."

"The company I work for leases cars for us. I'm a pharmaceutical salesman."

"A pharmaceutical salesman? I like drugs. I like grass, anyhow. I don't smoke much anymore."

I pick up a business card from beneath my pant leg and squint at the embossed printing of some physician's name. A wave of nausea causes me to lay the card down. "I don't need the heater on, if you're running it for me."

Cleve turns off the heater fan.

"How much farther?"

"Fifteen minutes."

We reach the end of the Costa Mesa Freeway, continue along Newport Boulevard, and stop at a red light. I spot a gas station a block ahead, on the right.

"I hate to tell you, but I've changed my mind about tonight. Would you mind letting me out at that service station?"

The light turns green, and we cross the intersection, drive another block and pass the station without slowing down. I point back with my thumb.

"You've changed your mind?"

"I'm sorry."

"Come to my place. We don't have to do anything."

"Maybe some other time."

We pass another gas station. I feel like I'm going to throw up.

Cleve pulls into a left turn lane, and we stop at a red light. "Where are we going?" I say.

"Where do you want to go?"

"Home."

"You're sure I can't talk you out of it?"

"Positive."

"Where's home?"

"Fullerton."

The light changes, and Cleve makes a U-turn around a center island. "You can drop me anywhere."

"Will you call the guy you were with?"

"I'll get a ride. Only I forgot my phone when I left home. Maybe I could use your phone?"

"I'll take you home."

"You don't have to."

"I'm apparently doing nothing else."

I see another gas station ahead. "Could we stop at that service station so I can use the men's room?"

"Are you feeling okay?" Cleve glances at me.

"Not entirely." I force a smile.

He moves two lanes to the right. "I'll gas up. Otherwise, they won't give you the key."

He pulls into the station and parks by a pump. I open the car door, lean out and heave. My barf splatters the cement as though flung from a pail. I heave a second time and a third. Slime hangs from my mouth as I fumble into my jeans pocket for a handkerchief. I taste and smell bourbon, almost as pure as it went down, along with partially digested chicken, fries, cherry pie à la mode.

After wiping my mouth with my handkerchief and mopping off the car door threshold, I look over at Cleve and smile.

"Feel better, handsome?" he says, grinning.

"Like a new man."

"Do you still want to use the bathroom?"

"Maybe we should shove off. People don't like you throwing up on their property. I learned that in college."

Cleve starts the car, and I close my door. We pull back onto Newport Boulevard and move into the middle lane.

"What do you want to do now?"

"Go home. You don't have to take me. I can call Dave—he'll come and get me."

"Did you guys have a fight?"

"Not exactly."

"I'll take you home. I feel like a drive."

We ride several blocks, past motels and bright fast-food joints, past a car repair shop, a tire outlet, a paint store, and other businesses closed for the night.

As we accelerate onto the freeway, I glance over at Cleve.

"Are you pissed at me?"

"No." He leans toward the dashboard and pushes a button. The country classic "Stand by Your Man" comes on. I smile as he looks aggravated and turns it off.

We roll up the Costa Mesa Freeway and over the interchange to the Santa Ana. I scoot down in my seat, lay my head back, and close my eyes.

"Are you feeling sick again?"

"A little. I'm okay. I was thinking about what a nice guy you are."

"Will you remember I'm a nice guy if things don't work out between you and what's-his-name?"

"I'll remember."

I reach over and place a hand on Cleve's leg. He covers it, squeezes my fingers, and then eases his hand into my lap.

He's massaging my erection through my jeans as we drive up Brookhurst. In the middle of our block, I tell him to make a U-turn and park in front of our house. I don't see any lights. Dave's in bed, I figure.

"Do you want to come in, and I'll make coffee?"

"Are you sure it'll be all right?"

"Dave's easygoing."

Unlocking the front door, I wonder if Dave's home.

Inside, a dim light shines from the hall on the other side of the living room.

Cleve follows me into the kitchen, and I flip on the ceiling lamp, pull the coffeemaker forward on the countertop. The room smells of ant spray. "Have a seat." I motion to the washing machine. Everything in my vision revolves slowly. Cleve leans against the dryer and unzips his jacket far enough to show a lot of curly black chest hair. I fill the coffeemaker and turn it on.

Dave appears in the kitchen doorway, dark green bikini underwear separating his muscled torso from his muscled legs. He glances at Cleve and then stares at me.

"This is my friend Cleve." I slur my words. "I got sick on the way to his house, and he brought me all the way back from Newport Beach. Stay up and have coffee with us. Cleve, this is Dave."

From a cabinet, I take three unmatched mugs and hold one after the other under the spout as coffee drips down. I slide the glass carafe under the machine to catch the rest.

"Cream or sugar, Cleve?"

"Black."

"Here you go."

The odor of coffee and ant spray makes me want to throw up again. "Let's go sit in the other room," I mumble, motioning before I follow Dave and Cleve into the living room. Dave switches on a black metal floor lamp at the end of our gray couch, sets his coffee on the arm of a matching chair, and goes into the bedroom. Cleve and I sit apart on the sofa, angled toward each other. Sipping coffee makes me feel sicker.

Dave comes out of the bedroom in jeans, pulling his zoo T-shirt over his head. He sits in the armchair and picks up his coffee mug.

Smiling as well as possible, I rise on shaky legs. "You guys get to know each other. I need to go to bed." I lean over, reach inside Cleve's jacket, and rub my fingers in his chest hair. "You deserve better than you got tonight."

"I'm not complaining."

I stagger through the hall into the bedroom, where the covers are pushed down on our bed. With my clothes on, I climb onto my side of the mattress and kiss the sheet on Dave's side, warm from his body. In college, I learned to lie on my back with one foot on the floor to keep the room from spinning, but our bed's too high. Bringing a knee up to my chest, I untie one of my retro black-and-brown saddle oxfords. I pull off the shoe, hold it out from the bedside, let go and listen to it thump on the wood floor. I raise my other knee, pull off my other shoe, and let go.

Light from the living room shines through the hall into the bedroom. Dave and Cleve talk. I don't listen to what they say, only to the murmur of their voices. I'm glad to be home in my own bed, with Dave no farther away than the next room. I don't want Dave to be farther away ever.

I drift off to sleep and wake when Dave comes to bed, however quiet he tries to be. "Are you all right?" he says. He kisses my forehead and helps me out of my T-shirt. He gets up and pulls off my socks and jeans and underpants. "I love you, Len," he says, after he lies back down.

"Want your biceps," I mutter, half-drunk, half-asleep. He understands and flexes an arm. I crawl on top of his chest and caress the mound of one of his biceps with both hands, running my nose and then my tongue over it. I nuzzle his armpit without letting go of his muscle. He strokes my hard cock and keeps flexing his biceps, making his arm pulse, until I come in his hand. Staying on top of him, I slide down to tongue the nub of his nipple and to raise my knee under his balls. I press my knee hard between his bulging bag and his anus, and he rides it as though he's sitting atop a post. He writhes against my knee, cups the back of my head with one hand, and hugs my face to his nipple. I stroke his cock. I look down and catch as much of his cream in my open mouth as I can.

I fall asleep on his chest, his arm around me.

3. SOMETHING GAINED, SOMETHING LOST

Pushing through the smudged glass door of the B and K Doughnut Shop, across the parking lot from Royal Books, I enter a warm room that smells sweet and stale, of coffee, grease, and sugar. Gray afternoon light dulls the bleached pink countertop and tables. A tiny Korean woman sells me two large coffees. After pouring sugar into one, I carry the paper cups to a table where Ian, in a black and orange rugby shirt, eats a jelly doughnut. Setting the coffee with sugar in front of him, I slide onto the hard plastic bench on the opposite side of the table. It's Tuesday; I haven't seen Ian since Friday. "Mind if I join you? I put sugar in the coffee for you."

He stares at me.

"Did you finish your Dostoevsky paper over the weekend?"

No answer.

I sip my coffee and keep talking. "I ran across *Sophie's Choice* in a stack of books under the bed Sunday and read all day. I loved it. I have the book in the office to give back to you." He loaned me *Sophie's Choice* before Christmas. I'd seen the movie on one of the historic film stations and mentioned I'd never read the book. "I liked the narrator trying to masturbate in the hotel room with his dad in the next bed."

Eyeing me with contempt, Ian shoves the last bite of his doughnut into his mouth.

"Look, Ian, if Dave broke a date with you, I didn't ask him to."

Picking up the white sack he used as a place mat, he scoots to the aisle on the bench seat.

"Don't blow me off, Ian. I'm warning you."

As he rises to his feet, I lunge against the table and grab him by the shirt collar.

"Let go of me, Lenny!"

"I'm not the trespasser in this situation, you son of a bitch!"

The tiny Korean woman stops making doughnuts and watches us.

I let go of his collar, and he steps away from the table, turns and walks out.

❖

I stay clear of everyone at the bookstore. I leave my office only for my lunch-hour trip to the gym. Otherwise, I sit at my desk and work on a drawing I started on my computer months ago, a draft for rearranging the store. Jane will never let me move everything around, and I doubt business would improve anyhow.

My office is far enough from the front windows that I don't notice afternoon fading until it's almost dark outside. Thinking about going home, making a note on my calendar for tomorrow, I realize Ian stands in my doorway. "I'll hunt for another job, Lenny."

"Hunt for another man while you're at it." Through the corner of my eye, I watch him glance over his shoulder at the counter. "You're a bastard, Ian."

He walks back to the register.

I grab my jacket, lock my door, and rush outside into a cool, light fog that feels almost soothing.

❖

As Dave and I wait for mugs of tea to steep after dinner, he pulls a folded slip of paper from his jeans pocket and hands it to me. I unfold the slip and see small neat printing in blue ink: Cleve Micolas and a phone number.

"That guy asked me to give you his number, so I'm giving it to you. I forgot I had it until I put on these jeans."

Dave turns and starts out of the kitchen.

"Don't you want your tea?" I ask.

He stops, and I hand him his chipped Georgetown University mug. He carries it into his den.

In our bedroom, I pick up a mystery lying open on the bed where I was reading before dinner. I wad up the slip of paper with Cleve's phone number on it and drop it into an empty wicker trash basket by the dresser.

❖

"Ian," I say, slipping up behind him in the sports aisle while afternoon sun floods through the bookstore's plate glass front. He looks anguished as he rises from stooping on one knee. I look anguished, too, I suppose. "Mai-Ly told me she isn't taking the internship, so she doesn't care about working evenings. Next week you can start Jack's shifts. You and I will overlap from five till six, one hour a day. We can stay out of each other's way." I wait, wanting to say more, wishing he would say something. Pulling a sports almanac forward on the shelf, I wipe dust off the top of it with my fingertip. "I don't know which I want more, Ian—to kick your ass or to fuck you."

Glancing at him, I shove the almanac back into place.

❖

Dave eats peanut butter on soda crackers in the kitchen as I walk by. Changing from my work clothes into jeans and a flannel shirt, I stare at the wadded note with Cleve's phone number lying on the bottom of the otherwise empty trash basket. I pick up the note, unwad it, and slip it into my wallet.

After carrying Cleve's number around for twenty-four indecisive hours, I call from my office, reach him on the first try, and invite myself to his place for a walk on the beach Saturday.

But when Saturday comes, I sit in my office fibbing over the phone, telling him I have to work for one of my staff who called in sick. Ian's handsome butt goes out the door into the sunny parking lot as I'm talking, and I wonder if he's on his way to meet Dave at the college. I finally admit to Cleve I'm afraid we'll end up in bed if I come to his place. I don't tell him I'm more afraid of all the men I'll go to bed with after him.

It's dark outside when I leave the bookstore. At home, Dave sweeps the living room. I lay my wallet and keys on the bedroom dresser. The bed is unmade. I try not to picture Ian in it. Valentine cards Dave and I gave each other are missing from the dresser, where they've stood since the holiday.

Dave moves his broom into the kitchen. I stand in its doorway. The clothes dryer runs. "I was planning to clean tomorrow," I say.

"I got tired of grading papers. How was your afternoon?"

"How was yours?"

He shrugs. "The short answers on the zoology test are terrible."

The broom handle taps against the bottom of a cabinet as he sweeps under it. He wears a tattered light blue knit shirt, the tail loose over gray sweats. He looks around the kitchen until he finds the dustpan on top of the refrigerator.

"What happened to our Valentine cards?" I say.

"They're in the drawer, with all our other cards. I was dusting. Why? I'll get them back out if you want."

"Whatever."

"What did you and that guy do?"

"Walked on the beach. Talked. Sucked dick." I point with my thumb to our bedroom. "Was Ian here?"

"Ian?"

"The bed's unmade."

Dave stops sweeping and holds the broom upright. "I took a nap, Lenny. I swear to you."

"You don't have to swear." I step in front of him and finger his nipples through the cloth of his shirt. "I didn't go to the beach. I called and broke the date, spent the afternoon at the bookstore talking to Rosie and Mai-Ly." I reach up under his shirt, and let the tips of my index fingers find the nubs of his nipples. After a moment, I lower one hand and grope under his tenting sweats, cup his balls. He loves his own big testicles so much I don't think he could love me if mine outsized his. He kisses me. I take his hand and lead him into our bedroom. We undress each other.

"Tell me what Ian does." I look up from between Dave's legs.

He stops moving his fingers through my hair. He holds his breath.

"Tell me, Dave. Does Ian do this?"

I take a testicle into my mouth. He watches and sighs in quiet rapture, like a cat purring. I let it slowly slip out.

"What else?" I crawl up, fold his arm, and kiss his biceps. "What about this?" I bend his other arm and kiss its mound of muscle.

Dave moans and hooks the crook of his arm around my neck. I slide down and gently take between my teeth the nub of a nipple. I tongue it and then move to his other one. "Ian loves your big nipples, doesn't he?" I move back and forth, from one to the other. "Does Ian sit on your cock?" I lubricate Dave and settle on his cock, my body a glove for it. He strokes my erection in spittle in his palm while he fingers my nipples with his other hand. "Tug on my tit the way you tug on Ian's," I pant. Dave watches my chest swell and opens his mouth to catch my cum. My first squirt leaves a line from his lower lip down his chin to his neck. My second burst lands in the hollow of his chest, and my third dribbles onto his six-pack. I lift my haunches, hugging his shaft with my anus and buttocks as I watch his face contort. Every muscle of his upper body bulges as he spasms inside me.

I lean down and kiss him. "I know how much Ian loves your big body," I whisper, "because I love it more."

We lie in each other's arms until we agree we're hungry for supper. It's dark outside by now. We both want to shower. I send him to the shower first and lie in bed listening to the water run, picturing him in its spray and thinking I can handle this.

After I shower, I join Dave, both of us in loosely sashed, matching robes my mom gave us for Christmas. We make lasagna and eat in the den, in front of the TV. We talk about streaming a movie but instead switch channels more than watch anything. I stare at a handsome middle-aged actor in a commercial. He tends a barbecue grill and says to his wife, "I can't believe a light beer tastes so good." On the phone with Cleve this afternoon, I asked if he'd ever been in love, and he told me about this ad, this actor, about seeing him on TV after not seeing him for six years.

❖

Honey—real name LuLing Sun—is a new hire I'm training. She's pretty and small, although I wouldn't call her petite as I would Mai-Ly. Honey is as outgoing as Rosie and even more animated, with waves of gold-streaked licorice hair bouncing over shoulders that rise and fall when she talks. Leaving her at the counter, I take a small screwdriver and adjust the book detector columns by the door. Jane arrives while I'm tinkering and stops in front of me, a pearl sweater chain draping her bosom, the empty sleeves of a beaded white silk cardigan hanging limp. When I introduced her to Honey on Friday, Jane smiled at me for the first time in days. New staff are welcome prey for Jane.

"Did you see the fog last night, Leonard?" She knows I hate being called Leonard. "I looked out the front of my house after *The Tonight Show* and couldn't see the road!"

"It was pea soup, all right."

"I was surprised it lifted so fast this morning. I meant to call and tell you I wouldn't be in till past noon."

She usually doesn't call, even if she's not coming. I couldn't care less. "I knew you'd be along."

She picks a thread off my tie and walks across the store. As I screw the book detector column back together, I watch Jane linger on the customers' side of the counter, gabbing at Honey. I walk past them to my desk and eat a burrito I bought on my way back from the gym.

I'm initialing invoices for the bookkeeper when Jane finally walks into our office, where our desks sit back to back, making us face each other over our laptop screens. I keep my eyes on my work as she stows her purse in her lower desk drawer, takes out a white plastic bottle, and begins rubbing lotion into her hands. "Honey's sweet," Jane says.

"She seems to be." I don't look up.

"She's homesick, so I'm taking her to lunch at the Brazilian restaurant on Euclid tomorrow." Jane always has a honeymoon period with a new hire. With Rosie and Mai-Ly, Jane turned bitchy within a month; with me, within a few months. Only Ian has managed to stretch the honeymoon period longer. I warned Honey. "Did you know she's Brazilian?" Jane asks me.

I nod. I read her job application, for Christ's sake. I needed her student visa to hire her.

Jane picks up a stack of envelopes from her desk. She insists on opening all first class mail, consequently first class mail can be held up for several days.

"You were wise to hire her, Lenny. I was afraid you were going to hire that boy you interviewed, and then we'd have the Ian problem all over again."

"What Ian problem?"

Jane plunges her letter opener into an envelope and pauses, her heavily made-up face twisted into a thinking mask. She's wearing new contact lenses, shockingly green. "Young men aren't as likely as young ladies to be comfortable working for someone of your persuasion."

"What are you getting at, Jane?"

"An attractive fellow like Ian can't help but be aware a man of your persuasion might have certain feelings for him. That's all."

"Are you saying Ian has a problem with me because I'm gay?"

"I'm sure he doesn't hold it against you. But that's why he wants Jack's hours."

"Says who?"

"Ian. He told Mai-Ly. Well, Lenny, you can't expect the whole world to embrace your lifestyle."

"Son of a bitch!" I bound to my feet. "This is such bullshit!"

Jane gawks up at me. "Leonard! I had no idea you'd overreact, or I wouldn't have brought the subject up!"

"I'm leaving for a while!"

I stomp through the store and out into the parking lot, hurl myself into my hatchback, and yank the door shut so hard the car rocks.

Rolling along Orangethorpe Avenue, I yell, "Fuck you, Ian!" over and over. I have no idea where I'm going.

On State College Boulevard, I realize I'm near Cal State and Dave's office.

Minutes later I cut across traffic and bump up the driveway of a coffee shop, park my car with a minor screech, and hustle indoors like a hit man late for an appointment. Muzak is playing as I grind my teeth following a hostess to one of many booths vacant during mid-afternoon. Long, low, tinted windows look out to sun glinting off passing traffic.

I ask for pie and coffee. The waitress recites my choices, and I stop her at lemon meringue.

I eat and drink, numbly aware I was on the verge of going to Dave's office and making a scene I would have regretted.

The waitress asks if I'd like more coffee, and I shake my head.

On my way out of the restaurant, I remember throwing up the last meal I ate here. It was the night I met Cleve.

Jane's gone when I get back to the bookstore. I sit at my desk and distract myself by searching online for authors I might invite for book signings. Until a year ago, we had two or three signings a month, something I instituted. I didn't get mainstream authors because our sales volume is too low to interest them or their publishers, but I booked locals, self-published or published by small presses. It's the only way an independent bookstore can stay in business, not that we sold enough books to secure our future, but we sold more than we have since we stopped signings.

We stopped because a children's author told a hectoring Christian mother she needed a nonstop electric dildo. Jane's lawyer settled out of court with some customers who threatened a lawsuit. He said there was no telling what damages a jury might award. Whenever I've mentioned reinstituting author signings, Jane gets scared in a sincere, unshowy way so unlike her normal histrionics it's stopped me from fighting her on the matter.

Ian rushes through the glass doors at quarter past five. I've been watching for him, and I bolt from my chair. I'm on his heels going into the stockroom.

"Sorry I'm late, Lenny. I took the freeway and got caught in a backup."

"You bastard!" I hiss, as the swinging door flaps at my back. "You told Mai-Ly you don't want to work with me because I'm *gay*?"

"I did not."

"The fuck you didn't! I've had it with you, Ian!"

"When Mai-Ly told me she wasn't taking the internship, I said that for *personal reasons* it would be better if you and I didn't work together. That's all!"

"What the fuck did you expect her to think?"

"It's not my fault."

"Nothing's ever your fault. Have you noticed that? You're such a bastard."

THE SHAPE OF THE EARTH

"Don't call me that."

"It's not my fault you're a bastard. I wish to hell you weren't!"

"How would you like someone calling you a faggot?"

He walks out of the stockroom. I'm trembling, more from fear than anger, knowing how close I came to slugging him in the mouth. I hit a guy in college and was nearly expelled. His parents threatened to sue my mom.

When I come out of the stockroom, Ian leans over the counter talking to Mai-Ly, behind the cash register. I slip around the counter and step into my office. A moment later, I see Ian head up the romance aisle, a box of books on his shoulder. Romances are our best sellers. I thought I could get graphic books to move, but a comics store in town has that business.

Ian never knew his father. He told Rosie his father "abrogated," I remember.

With one arm in my leather jacket, I start for the front door. Halfway there, I veer to the romance aisle and watch Ian, squatting as he stickers and shelves books, unaware of me behind him. "You're a self-serving shit, Ian. That's all I meant when I called you a bastard."

He looks up, over his shoulder. I turn and walk out.

❖

Honey's with me at the bookstore's plate glass windows watching a downpour flood the parking lot. In the two weeks since Ian and I stopped speaking to each other, rain has soaked Southern California, now rife with mudslides. Through the blurry windows Jane comes into view, rushing along the unsheltered storefront, struggling to keep her clear umbrella from blowing inside out. The umbrella matches a clear scarf over her blond head, a clear raincoat over her brown suit, and clear boots over her orange high-heels. She's clutching an orange purse to her bosom, like a quarterback protecting the football. I grin at Honey. "Here comes the Plastic Bubble Woman."

Holding the door open for Jane, I grab her umbrella and lower it. She's laughing good-naturedly. Honey's laughing at what I said.

"A little wet out there, Jane?" I ask.

"It was only sprinkling when I left my house."

Through the corner of my eye, I watch Rosie hang up the phone at the register. I'm glad Rosie hung up. Jane nags me about Rosie talking to her friends.

Somber-faced, Rosie gathers her long auburn hair behind her neck and stares across the floor, at the three of us by the door. "That was Ian on the phone. His mother died last night. Don't ask me how he's doing. You know he'd fall on a sword before he'd show any emotion. Melinda's with him."

Jane unsnaps her scarf, removes it, and shakes beads of water off the clear plastic onto a doormat over the store's aqua carpet. "I'd better call him. He won't know the first thing about arranging a funeral, and that silly Melinda will know even less. She cracked one of my Royal Doulton teacups running it through the dishwasher when Ian stayed at my place. Poor Ian offered to pay for it. I didn't have the heart to tell him how much vintage Royal Doulton costs."

❖

When I come in the back door of the house from work, Dave's on the phone, laughing. "Mom actually said that? What'd Dad say?" He's talking to one of his sisters—probably

Diane, in Chicago. He and Diane laugh a lot. I head into the bathroom and piss. Dave hangs up as I come back into the kitchen. "Diane says Mom and Dad won't be here in April. Mom can only get a couple days off."

Dave's mom, with her sweep of platinum hair and halting Kentucky drawl, reminds me of a born-again Doris Day on Valium. I smile.

"Mom was okay last time they were here," he says, a little defensively.

"She was fine, we had fun. We'll be in Cincinnati in July. Maybe that's soon enough to see your folks, with things the way they are."

I lean against the stove, Dave leans against the counter, and we stare at the floor. We have something to hide from our parents. We're not used to hiding.

"Do you know about Ian's mom?" I say.

"He called this afternoon."

"Everyone from the bookstore is going to the funeral. Are you?"

"I teach at eleven on Thursdays. It'll be okay if I don't go."

"Did you ever meet his mom?"

He shakes his head.

"You've never been to his house?"

He shakes his head again.

It figures Ian wouldn't take Dave home with his alcoholic mother there. That means Dave and he have sex on a narrow futon I bought at a garage sale a few years ago and carted to Dave's office for his after-lunch naps.

"I met Ian's mother once," I say, "when I gave him a ride home. I bet you've been to Jane's house, haven't you?"

Dave looks out the back door window and shrugs.

"Sorry I asked. It doesn't matter."

I'm surprised I saw him and Ian at the doughnut shop by the college when Ian was house-sitting for Jane.

❖

I think of Dave and Ian at Jane's house as I ride in the front of Jane's Cadillac and watch the windshield wipers glide back and forth. Jane thinks Ian has a problem with *me* because *I'm* homosexual. The irony is too much. We pass Ian's house, a stucco rancher similar to Dave's and mine, only with paint peeling off the wood trim. On the patchy lawn, two straggly Australian ferns look like giant mutant spiders. I mentally replay a rainy night when Ian's old Ford wouldn't take a jump-start, and I drove him home and watched him pad up the driveway, wet shoes and socks dangling from his hand. At the end of the block, Jane turns into the parking lot of a Church of God that could be a Sizzler or a Bonanza—it's a steak house–sized building with a similarly low peaked roof. She talks as she shuts off the engine. She's been talking since we left the bookstore. With Ian's mother's death, Jane has become a nonstop verbal encyclopedia of alcoholism and diabetes.

Mai-Ly, in the back seat, is silent.

Not anxious to go to a funeral, I sit with my hand on the car door handle while Jane puts her keys in her purse and examines her face in the mirror. "I surely hope, Leonard, your experience with Ian taught you a lesson."

"My experience with Ian? Jane, if this has anything to do with what you were saying on the drive here, I wasn't listening to a word, so I don't know what the hell you're talking about."

We get out of the car and glare at each other across the Cadillac's wet roof, Jane under her clear umbrella.

"We're here for a funeral, buster. Don't try to start an argument with me."

I'd slap her face if she were within reach. The thought sends a shock wave through my bowels. In thirty years of living, I've come to realize my temper is my worst enemy. It can make me do self-destructive things I'm ashamed of later. I look helplessly at Mai-Ly, who lowers her eyes to the puddled pavement and closes her car door.

I follow the two women to the church and into the nearly empty sanctuary, more like a small auditorium, with a speckled brown linoleum floor and Samsonite folding chairs. Jane stops just inside the doorway, to wait for Jack and his wife to arrive. Mai-Ly and I walk halfway up the aisle, the tapping of our hard soles the only sound other than rain drumming on the roof. We sit by Rosie, who scoots over two chairs on an otherwise empty row.

Ian sits in the front row, between Melinda and a pudgy-necked man whose white shirt collar is too tight above his sheeny blue suit coat. Staring at the back of Ian's head of fine black hair, I remember how close I came to slugging him, and feel another shock wave in my bowels.

I get up from my chair and walk as quietly as I can to the back of the church.

Jane watches me approach, a look of disdain on her face. "Where are you going?"

"To move my bowels." I smile when she winces.

Sitting on a toilet in a wing of Sunday school rooms, I think of my father dying of lung cancer my junior year of college. I still have fantasies in which Pop wasn't in and out of mental hospitals most of my growing-up years. As a preteen, I had fantasies where Pop and I went camping in the Piney Woods above Houston, skinny-dipping in a mythical pond. In every variation of that fantasy, I wound up in a fight with some kid who came along, besting him, proving I was a he-man boy. Not that Pop was a he-man dad, as my fantasy father was. Pop wasn't big, not broad or muscular, not as tall as I grew to be.

I'm sorry for Ian. He had an alcoholic mom and no dad. I have a super mom, and I had a dad who loved me, wherever his mind went.

I slip back into the sanctuary, into my aisle seat by Mai-Ly. The pudgy-necked man is standing in front of the casket mouthing homilies punctuated by *dearly beloved*s. His cloying eyes stare out from below his gray pompadour, and a line of spittle tethers his parted ruby lips. After he asks the small congregation to rise and bow our heads, he says a prayer and then returns to his seat next to Ian. The twenty or so of us in the congregation resettle in our chairs, while a gale flings rain against the amber glass windows. The funeral is over, I hope.

Ian stands in front of the casket. He looks composed but haggard. He wears a gray suit, a white shirt, and a maroon tie. I've never seen him dressed up before, and I get a boner.

"My mom made me promise to sing 'The Battle Hymn of the Republic' today. When I was little, she had a Judy Garland disc that I sang and danced to. I thought the chorus was 'Laurie, Laurie, how's it to ya?' I have no idea who I thought Laurie was or what I thought the song was about. Here goes."

He sings a cappella, with little expression or movement. His voice is strong and melodic. On the chorus, he changes the words to "Laurie, Laurie, how's it to ya?" He raises his arms above his head and shifts his weight back and forth from leg to leg, swaying his hips without moving his feet, the way a child might dance.

I hear Rosie snuffle, on Mai-Ly's other side, as I force back my own tears. I suspect Rosie and I are the only ones in the room who know Judy Garland is a gay icon.

❖

Saturday afternoon, our sixty-year-old silver pixie-haired bookkeeper, Helen, leaves my office filled with tobacco smoke, illegal on the premises. She's more politically conservative than Jane, yet likeable because she isn't an elitist. Helen prepares monthly spreadsheets for Jane's accountant, a man too polite to say what I believe he thinks, which is that Royal Books should close down. Helen and her cigarettes normally work at home, but she and I met at the bookstore late this morning to talk about integrating our inventory and accounting systems.

Lingering alone in my office, I watch Ian help a woman at the register, picture him singing, "Laurie, Laurie, how's it to ya?" I didn't see him yesterday. Jane was giving me her silent treatment, knocking things around on her desk to show how irritated she was with me. When the sun appeared between the clouds for the first time in a week, I got up and went home—which I'm about to do now, although it's cloudy again.

I stick my arms into my worn leather jacket and grab the gray fedora I bought at a flea market during college. Ian's with another customer and doesn't see me wave good-bye. His shift ends a few minutes from now. I wonder if Dave will be home when I get there.

Rain falls lightly, and I stop outside the store to zip my jacket. A handful of seagulls glide in circles as I cross the puddled parking lot to the doughnut shop's takeaway window. Standing under the strip mall overhang, I sip coffee and divide my attention between the gulls and the cars coming and going. Carrying my half-full cup, I start across the misty lot to my hatchback, nosed to the edge of the blacktop near Harbor Boulevard. I'm almost to my car when I see the flat rear tire. "Mother *fuck*." I stop and stare at my disabled vehicle. "*Ah, mother fuck!*" With all my might, I fling my lidded cup at the wheel. It hits the rim and bursts like a water balloon. I turn my back in disgust and see Ian standing twenty yards away.

"Do you want help changing the tire?" he yells.

I'm too pissed to answer.

He circumvents a puddle and walks over to me. "I'll give you a hand."

"I need more than a hand. Someone stole my spare. *God damn it!*" Dave said this would happen if I put off buying a new spare.

"I'll take you to get a tire."

"I don't want to buy a motherfucking tire. I'm too pissed at the moment, in case you haven't noticed. I hate dealing with garages. I don't know a blessed thing about cars."

"Neither do I."

"I'll think about tires tomorrow."

"How about a ride home?"

"Thanks. I would fucking love a ride home."

Ian's car is parked several empty spaces from mine. I walk through puddles, while he walks around them, and I'm first to reach his car, my deck shoes and sockless feet soaked.

"The door isn't locked," he says as he gets in.

I take off my fedora to duck under the frame, while he moves a pile of books from the threadbare seat on the passenger side. The wipers lie across the windshield at odd angles; when he starts the car, the wiper on my side moves faster than the one on his.

"I have no idea when my spare was stolen," I tell Ian. "I waxed my car Thanksgiving weekend and when I lifted the panel, the tire wasn't there."

Rain falls harder as we drive up busy Harbor Boulevard and turn left onto a block of Valencia Drive lined with jacaranda trees and bungalows, among Fullerton's oldest neighborhoods.

I wish Ian hadn't seen me throw my coffee cup at my car.

Beyond an elementary school set amid boxy stucco houses like Dave's and mine, we turn left on Brookhurst. We stop in the middle of the second block in front of our house. Our lawn needs mowing. The grass has grown a couple of inches with all the rain. I try to think of some parting quip to make before I get out, so Ian won't think I'm such a hothead.

"Thanks for the ride," I mumble.

"Sure. Can I come in for a few minutes?"

I watch the windshield wipers flop back and forth. Dave might be home. I'm not in the mood to face Dave and Ian together.

"Or can we go somewhere for a cup of coffee, Lenny? I don't feel like being alone, if you have a little time to kill."

I try to remember whether Dave said he was going to campus this afternoon. Screw it, I decide. "You can come in."

Through a downpour, we dash up the walk to the small cement porch. Rain sizzles, loud and fragrant. Runoff streams from the roof overhang and splashes the muddy ground as I unlock the door and we duck inside. "Anyone home?"

Dave doesn't answer.

I toss my jacket and hat on the washing machine. The house smells of last night's salmon. We couldn't grill outdoors because of rain. A few dozen ants crawl on the sink counter, and I wipe them up with a paper napkin. I grab towels from the bathroom and my old Haverford College sweatshirt from the bedroom, and we dry our heads and hands.

"Give me a minute while I change. That sweatshirt's clean, if you want to wear it."

I slosh back to the bedroom in my waterlogged shoes, strip, and put on beige shorts and a gold cashmere sweater I wear as a shirt. It has holes in the armpits. I join Ian in the living room. He wears my sweatshirt and has taken off his wet sneakers and socks. Glimpsing his light tan bare feet on the wood floor, I feel my heart bump. I kneel to turn on the gas in our small fireplace, while Ian browses a bookcase. He picks up Dave's tome, *The Interaction of Western Diamondback Rattlesnakes.*

"I'll show you a picture in there."

Ian hands me the book as I rise to my feet.

I find a photo of two rattlers squaring off, their back halves coiled in dust, front halves raised vertically a yard off the ground. "Two males about to fight. They wrap around each other and flop all over hell."

"I never thought about how snakes fight." He stares at the picture after I pass back the book. Eventually he returns it to the shelf, keeping his finger on the spine, by Dave's name. He cocks his head at me.

"It's Dave's," I confirm.

I fill the coffeemaker with water. "I'm sorry about your mom, Ian. I know how depressed I got when my dad died."

"It feels strange. There's no one to take care of but myself."

"Do you have any aunts or uncles?"

"The closest thing to family we ever had was a Mrs. O my mom worked for in a laundry in Dublin. She stayed with us on a trip over here when I was ten."

The kitchen smells less of salmon and more of coffee. Before the pot is full, I pick it up and pour a mug for Ian, dripping coffee singeing the machine's metal warming plate.

He carries his coffee into the living room, and I follow. He glances around the room, looking at the bare walls Dave and I keep meaning to hang something on, at our dull couch and chair, at the bookcase, the fireplace.

"Curious about Dave's habitat?" I say.

Ian uses his free hand to pick up an open book that lay facedown on the couch. He stares at the title, *Woman in the*

Dark. "I've read this. A lady I did yard work for in high school had it." He keeps my place with a finger.

"Maybe that was her copy. I got it at the Goodwill."

"She moved years ago."

Still standing, we stare at each other. "You didn't answer my question. Curious about where Dave lives?"

Ian steps closer and kisses me. Only our lips touch, and he steps back.

"Friends, Lenny?"

"It's easier for you."

He flips to the front of the book. "Do you have other Dashiell Hammett mysteries?"

"I have most of them."

Ian follows me into the bedroom. "I've never seen a bed that high," he says, while I peruse a bookcase.

"We got it from Dave's grandparents." I find six Dashiell Hammett mysteries, carry them in a stack to the living room, and drop them on the couch.

We drink coffee and talk about old mysteries, my mind never wandering far from our kiss. Daylight fades, and the fire appears brighter. I turn down the flame because the room is warm. Switching on the lamp by the couch, I realize Dave could get home any minute.

I carry our empty mugs to the kitchen. Ian follows and talks about Cain's *Double Indemnity*—the difference between the book and the forties movie. He glances at the half-full coffee pot as I put our mugs in the dishwasher. "You're welcome to borrow those Dashiell Hammett mysteries if you want."

"I guess I should be going, huh?"

He removes my sweatshirt, and I watch his small, taut nipples as they disappear beneath the green sweater and T-shirt he takes from the back doorknob and pulls on as one garment.

"Are you seeing Melinda this evening?"

"She's in Indio, for her father's birthday. We're just friends, in case you've wondered. What are you guys doing tonight?"

"Nothing special."

"Do you want company? You asked me to dinner a while ago."

I shove my hands into my pockets and glance at the dark windowpane streaked with rain. Ian picks up his shoes and socks and leads the way into the living room. He opens the front door, letting in a draft of earthy air and the sound of rainwater singing through a drainpipe that runs down the front of the house.

"You can stay, Ian." Reaching past him, I shove the door closed. "Make yourself at home while I start dinner. Dave'll be here soon."

Avoiding Ian's eyes, I head into the kitchen. As I wait for water to boil, I realize how nervous I am. The pot hisses and trembles, and I turn down the flame because it's too soon to put in the pasta. Seeing Ian isn't in the living room, I go find him by a guest room bookcase, an open Bible in his hands. "You're a Pentecostalist?"

"We just went to that church because it was down the street. I quit going during high school." His eyes return to the Bible. "It's interesting to see how different the translations are."

"I bought that Bible for a lit class in college."

We return to the living room. He asks if he can turn up the fire, and I nod. When he kneels on all fours at the hearth, I watch the soles of his bare feet and a sliver of his lightly tanned back as his sweater and T-shirt ride up.

On web radio, over my phone lying on the kitchen counter, a comedian talks about his cat's sex life while I work at peeling and slicing tomatoes and cucumbers. Ian sits on the couch reading, the gas fire blazing across the room from him. I lay down my knife and slip through the living room and hall and into the bathroom. Coming back, I see Ian's left foot propped over his knee and watch him wag its smooth sole as I cross the room.

I'm fumbling salad greens on plates when the back door opens and I jump, knocking half of one salad on the counter.

"It's raining like hell!" Dave says, dropping his gym bag and briefcase on the floor. Water drips off his black windbreaker, his wet face partially covered by the hood. The knees of his jeans are soaked, and his boots make a squishing sound as he shifts his weight from foot to foot. "These boots are shot. I might as well be walking around outside in my socks." He pushes the hood off his head, pecks me on the lips, and then he eyes the three salad plates on the counter. "Someone's coming to dinner?"

"I had a flat tire, and Ian gave me a ride home."

With a start, Dave glances into the living room. "Ian," he calls. "How are you holding up?"

"All right. I knew my mom could die anytime."

Ian gets up from the couch and steps into the kitchen doorway. He locks his hands behind his neck and stretches, looking from Dave to me.

The guy on the radio jokes about his penis as though it's a creature apart from him.

"I'll open wine," Dave says.

While the pasta boils, we sip merlot and avoid more than a glance at each other as the comedian tries to milk his tenth high school reunion for laughs.

We eat in front of the fireplace, sitting with legs folded, Ian between Dave and me, faces aglow from the blaze, the only light in the room. We talk about the Academy Awards coming up soon, but none of us knows exactly when. I barely follow the conversation, only fully conscious of Ian caressing the ball of my foot with his toes.

I set my empty plate at my side, take Ian's plate, and stack it on mine. Glancing past him, I meet Dave's eyes in the firelight as I wrap my arm around Ian's waist. Ian turns to me, and I kiss him. He pulls up my T-shirt, and I raise my arms and shrug it off. I help him tug off his own sweater and shirt. Dave rises to his knees and scoots behind us and caresses our bare backs while we kiss.

On our high double bed, I slide my fingers between the toes of Ian's raised feet while Dave unrolls a condom along me and slathers it with KY. I want to tell Dave I love him. In my mind, I do tell him.

I want to go slow with Ian, make it last, but I've wanted him for too long.

Dave goes slow. I've never watched my cowboy's backside while he's fucking. I hang on to his balls like I've slipped off a ledge and grabbed them to keep from falling.

After Dave comes, Ian needs barely more than my breath to erupt in my mouth.

We lie against each other, Ian in the middle of the double bed, dim light shining into the room from the hall. Dave and I take turns kissing him, while rain patters the roof in bursts like handfuls of thrown pebbles. I slide down on Ian until he pulls me up and raises his legs again. This time I go slow while he arches his back and moans *Jesus* over and over.

Exhausted and content, I fall asleep.

When I wake, Dave holds my hand. "We're moving to the sofa bed, so we'll have more room." I let Dave lead me to our queen-sized sofa bed, opened out in the guest room, with Ian curled on his side. I spoon against him, kissing his shoulders and neck. He reaches back, takes hold of me, while Dave lies in front of him, kissing him. I feel like I'm in a dream.

❖

I wake at dawn, and Ian is blowing Dave while Dave calls him lover. I pretend I'm still asleep. After they both come, they fall back asleep without knowing I was ever awake. I get up, shower, sit on the couch, and read the paper on my phone. They get up and shower together.

Dave—naked and goose bumped—makes pancakes. Ian and I, in sweaters and jeans, sit on the washer and dryer. We're sleepy. I hope Ian's asshole isn't sore. Dave talks about teaching, but his mind is on exhibiting himself. He slips a thumb under his puffy scrotum as though scratching, but I know he's showing off his balls. He flicks the protuberant nub of a taut nipple with his thumb.

Sitting on the living room floor in front of the blazing fireplace, we eat.

Ian needs to go home and change clothes before he opens the bookstore. I stand back and watch Dave's muscular buttocks clench as he kisses Ian at our front door. They exchange a few murmured words I can't make out.

After Ian's gone, Dave and his half-mast cock stumble back to our high double bed. I peel off my sweater and jeans and crawl in beside him under the comforter. Watching him fall asleep, I feel the warmth of his body, smell the coffee and maple syrup on his breath.

I want to wake him and ask how he felt after he had sex with Ian for the first time. Whether he felt he'd lost something. I wonder if I'm feeling what young girls feel after they lose their virginity. I want back my three, almost four, years of monogamy, so they can become ten years and twenty years.

I slip off the bed, shut myself in the bathroom, and sit on the closed toilet wondering if I'm going to cry. I worked so hard learning not to cry as a teenager. I cried so much two years ago when Michael, my lover during high school and closest friend since, died in a car wreck. His death still doesn't seem real to me.

When no tears come, I get up from the toilet and slip back into bed to watch Dave sleep.

4. BALTIMORE

I stand on the customer's side of the counter and over my shoulder watch our only patron of the past half hour carry his purchase out the door and into the sunny parking lot. I turn to Rosie on the stool behind the cash register. "Did I ever tell you I was going to be an architect?"

"*Querido*, architects are *so* sexy."

I lean across the counter to talk confidentially, as though we aren't alone. "The man you just waited on reminds me of an architect I worked for my junior year of college. He and I wound up having sex. After we'd done it a few times, he said he was in love with me, and I freaked and quit my job. Besides a wife, he had a baby."

What I really want to tell Rosie is that I slept with Ian.

"So, *querido*, you gave up a career in architecture because you fucked some guy?"

"I was just a boy Friday at the firm. But I took an architecture class after I quit."

"I think you're a natural for architecture. I can picture your interview spread in *Architectural Digest*—a photo of you looking artsy-serious, the top buttons of your golf shirt undone to show some luscious blond chest hair."

"You're such a loose woman, Rosie. You're almost as bad as I am."

I wink at her and walk around the counter and into my office.

Rosie's still sitting on the stool by the register when Ian arrives for his evening shift. I watch them exchange a few words and then watch Ian go into the popular fiction aisle. I step out of my office, scoot around the counter, and stroll into the aisle where Ian tidies up the shelves and puts books back in order by author. Blood flows to my crotch. "I've been looking forward to seeing you all day," I say to his profile.

He works on a lower shelf. "I can't believe how fast books get out of order."

"Saturday night was great."

"Lenny, can we not talk about it?"

"No one can hear us."

"I don't want to talk about it."

"Why?"

"I just don't."

"What's the matter?"

"Nothing. I don't want to be some couple's plaything."

"You're not a plaything, any more than I'm a plaything or Dave is."

"Bullshit. You guys have a relationship."

"Ian, what do you want? We all had a great time."

"At least let me catch my breath, would you, Lenny?"

"Sure, whatever. I didn't mean to hassle you."

Feeling rebuked, I watch his tanned, quick-moving fingers. I inhale his clean shampoo scent and mosey back to my office.

We nod to each other, nothing more, during our next couple of daily one-hour overlaps.

Thursday, ready to leave, I stop just beyond my door. Ian

sits on the stool by the register. "Jane mentioned you got into the Johns Hopkins PhD program with full funding?"

He nods.

"Congratulations, Ian." I try to overlook the fact that he told Jane before he told me.

"Thanks."

I step closer to him. "I had no idea you applied to schools outside the LA area."

"I applied to Hopkins on a whim. I never thought I'd go, because of my mom."

"For what it's worth, Dave and I liked living in the East. We'd probably still be in DC if he'd gotten a teaching job there."

"I've lived here all my life. Everyone I know is here. What would I do in Baltimore?"

He stares out the plate glass window to the parking lot. The bright March evening is cold and gusty. People wear jackets as they climb in and out of cars. Women cup hands around hairdos.

I move close enough to talk in Ian's ear. "Personally, I hope you don't go to Hopkins. I enjoyed bed last weekend *way* too much." I don't want him to feel hassled, so I turn and head for the door and out to my car.

❖

At home, as I refill our wineglasses over supper, I mention to Dave that Ian got into Hopkins. "Should we invite him for dinner Saturday, have a little celebration?" I say.

"I think he has plans with Melinda. Anyhow, he heard from Hopkins a while ago."

I wait for Dave to suggest another night to invite Ian over, but he doesn't. The fact that Ian knew about Hopkins even before yesterday and didn't mention it to me leaves me feeling less important to him than I'd like to be.

❖

I'm nodding off for an afternoon nap on the couch, the Sunday paper open on my phone lying on my sweater-clad chest. A hardback mystery nests facedown on the floor in a spine-breaking position. The book was a months-late birthday present from Sandy. Dave and I had dinner with her last night.

I'm startled awake by Dave carrying his briefcase from his den. "I'll be back in plenty of time for supper."

I blink up at him. He couldn't look more guilty if he were on his way to fuck all the boys in the freshmen class. I wonder if he'll have the balls to leave the house.

He walks into the kitchen, and I hear the back door open and close.

"You motherfucker," I mutter.

Sitting up on the couch, I fling my book against the wall with all my might. It thuds and bounces to the floor. I stare at a bent corner of the cover and think of Sandy hugging me good night and whispering, "Hang in there, babe."

I close the living room drapes, strip off my clothes, and fondle myself as I walk into the bedroom. Sifting through a junk drawer in our nightstand, I find an ancient little brown bottle of amyl nitrate. In Dave's den, sitting at his desk as I sniff from the bottle, I picture his big naked body on top of Ian. I see Ian stroke his own cock while Dave's slides in and out of Ian's ass. The amyl nitrate makes me so hard, I feel like I'm nothing but one giant dick. Dave and Ian kiss as they're about to come in my fantasy. I inhale more from the small bottle and gush all the way up to my chin, a real geyser.

Falling back in Dave's chair, I shut my eyes and take

deep breaths to slow my racing heart. I should have thrown out the amyl nitrate when Dave and I agreed we wouldn't use it anymore. Motionless, one hand frozen around my waning instrument, I gaze at an Auto Club map of California thumbtacked above Dave's desk. On a corner of his desktop, a color photo of a coral snake catches my eye. I pick it up. Below it lies a newsletter page of job ads, one for an assistant biology professor at the University of Baltimore. Scanning the page, I notice another ad for a visiting zoology professor at George Washington University, an hour from Baltimore.

I carry the amyl nitrate bottle to the kitchen trash and drop it into an empty milk carton, so Dave won't see it. I swallow an old Valium and consider calling Sandy, but I don't want to hear myself telling her I'm afraid Dave's going to leave me.

❖

Warming up on a stationary bicycle at the gym, I spot a guy named Tony doing leg presses among the usual lunch-hour crowd. Tony's my size and build, a little younger than I am, and handsome, with a Roman soldier's curly dark hair. He and his wife are trying to have a baby. Tony sees me but pretends he doesn't.

I work through my routine—stretches, weights, crunches, and stair climber. With my tank shirt glued to my torso in sweat, I head into the locker room, where Tony's stripping next to my locker, his jock strap and trunks pushed to his knees. Seeing me, he nearly trips grabbing a towel to wrap around his waist. I spin the dial on my combination lock.

"It's not my fault locker rooms aren't unisex, Tony."

"Huh?"

I stop on a wrong number but close enough that my lock opens anyhow.

"Because I ogle women?" he asks.

I strip, grab my towel, and slam my locker door. Giving Tony a disgusted look, I step past him into the shower room, where three showers run behind closed curtains. Tony follows on my heels.

"You're an asshole, Tony," I say over my shoulder.

"*What?*"

"You heard me."

Hanging my towel on a hook, I step into a shower, pull the translucent curtain, and start the water, standing out of its cold spray while it warms up. I see Tony's shape through the plastic. "I thought we were *friends*!" I holler.

He moves away, and I hear another shower start.

I admit I've glanced at Tony's uncut meat while he towels his face dry, and I find his tattooed calves and buttocks sexy as hell. Dave once asked me if he should get tattooed, and I said I liked him free and clear, which I do. Still, Tony's tattoos make me want to raise my legs for him. Why should it matter to Tony?

I caught him ogling the backsides of women on treadmills, and we laughed about that. We talked about how much willpower being faithful takes. Then one afternoon, Tony said we should get together for dinner with our other halves, and I told him my other half wasn't a wife. Since then I've gotten the same cold shoulder I sometimes get from Ian, only Tony's reason isn't duplicitous. He's just homophobic.

No showers are running when I step out onto the puddled gray tile. The room is warm and smells of ammonia. I dry in solitude, staring at flakes of electric yellow paint peeling off walls powder blue beneath.

As I pad out of the shower room, a man in suit trousers and tasseled loafers rolls deodorant under an arm at a counter of sinks with mirror above it. He looks my way and smiles. I don't recognize him at first.

"*Cleve*—what are you doing here?"

"Working out."

"I've never seen you here before."

"I've been here a few times, when I was calling on accounts nearby."

"It's good to see you."

"Likewise."

I unwrap the towel from around my waist and toss it in a tub.

"So how have you been?" I say as his hazel eyes make a quick tour of my body.

"All right. How about you?"

"Same. Nothing new."

A couple of fully clothed guys walk between us on their way out. I step into the aisle by my locker, where Tony tucks a striped, button-down shirt into blue trousers. Cleve steps into the next aisle. He and I can still see each other in the mirror.

Tony slams his locker and squeezes past me as I open mine.

Cleve, knotting a tie, steps to the sinks to be closer to the mirror. Naked, I join him and comb my hair. "I didn't see you upstairs, Cleve."

"I saw you."

"Why didn't you say something?"

"You were working hard. It was enough of a pleasure just to watch you." He pulls off the tie he just put on. "I don't need a tie. I'm through calling on accounts today."

He goes back to his locker. I watch him pick up his gym bag from the bench.

"Give me a minute, Cleve. I'll walk out with you."

I stuff away my workout clothes, pull on my underpants, trousers, socks, and shoes. Carrying my shirt over one shoulder, rather than wearing it, I follow him from the locker room and past the reception desk. As we step outdoors, the white walls of a Moorish medical building glare from the front of the parking lot. Cleve pulls sunglasses from his shirt pocket. I lower mine from atop my head. "How about a cup of coffee, Cleve?"

"If you want."

"Maybe my place? It's only ten minutes from here if we jump on the freeway. I won't disappoint you this time."

He stares at the medical building a moment. "Are you sure you want to do this?"

"I'm sure." I motion to my car. "The silver hatchback's mine. Follow me."

"I remember where you live, but…"

"But nothing. See you in a few minutes."

Pulling onto the freeway, I watch in my rearview mirror as Cleve follows.

Near the house, I stop at a drugstore. Cleve rolls into the parking space next to mine. "I'll be right back," I shout.

Shirtless at the pharmacy counter, I buy a package of condoms and wink at the unsettled pharmacist.

At home, I call the bookstore and tell Honey my car overheated and I'm waiting for a gas station mechanic to look at it.

Unbuttoning and untucking Cleve's shirt, I rub my fingers in the black hair funneling down his chest and hard belly. He smells like towels fresh from the dryer at the gym. I reach to unbuckle his belt, but he stops me. "Is there any chance what's-his-name could come home?"

"He teaches on Monday afternoons." I unzip Cleve's fly. "Fuck Dave anyhow. You have the balls to hang a pair of horns on him, don't you, Cleve?" I cup Cleve's testicles in my hand.

He smiles. "I have the balls."

I lead him by the head of his cock to the high double bed. We strip and climb into it. I blow him till he's almost ready to come, and then I sheathe him in a rubber and ask whether he wants me on my stomach or back. He shoves me down face up, and I raise my legs. His thrusts are firm, his cock nudging my prostate until I writhe. Every muscle in his face strains as he holds off his orgasm. "Here I come, Lenny." I feel his cock flex, his whole body shudder. I squirt into his chest hair, and with my fingertips spread my cum throughout that tangled jungle.

We lie kissing.

I mention I should get back to the bookstore eventually, and he gets up and crosses the hall to the bathroom. "I probably shouldn't flush this condom," he calls, "but you might not want it in the trash."

"Leave it on the toilet tank. I'll take care of it."

I listen as he pisses. Sitting on the side of the bed, I try not to panic about what I've done.

As Cleve steps from the bathroom into the hall, I hear our back door open. Cleve freezes. Dave's briefcase thumps on the kitchen floor. "Shit!" Dave shouts, and the back door slams.

From the hall, Cleve stares into the bedroom at the closed, sun-drenched drapes. We hear Dave's car idle and drive away.

"Did you plan this?" Cleve says.

I shake my head. "Dave saw you?"

"If he did, I didn't see him. I don't care if you did plan it." Cleve crosses the room and kisses me and pulls me from the side of the bed into its middle. His cock juts out so hard it could be carved from stone. "Let him come back and see me taking you."

I whisper, "Fuck my mouth, Cleve," as he climbs in bed. I prop my head against a pillow, and he straddles my torso.

I watch his chest swell and show all its muscle, and then I taste his semen. His body doubles in two, his biceps and pecs envelop my face. He recovers enough to scoot down on the bed and wrap a hand around my bone. I stop him. "I'm all right."

He looks at the bathroom.

"Jump in the shower if you like, Cleve."

We kiss, and he climbs off the bed.

While the shower runs, I stroke myself off picturing his swollen chest as he came in my mouth. In my private aftermath, I lie marveling at the effect rising to orgasm has on a man's chest. I imagine lining up all the well-built men in the world and staring up at their bare chests while I suck them off man after man.

I'm pissing when Cleve opens the shower curtain. "How about a sandwich?" I say. Neither of us ate lunch. I don't want to appear anxious for Cleve to go, although I am.

He leans against the stove in his boxer shorts and watches me, naked, take cold cuts out of the refrigerator and set up coffee. I try to ignore Dave's gym bag, which sits just inside the back door.

"Are you sure you don't want me to leave before he comes home again?" Cleve says, following my eye.

"Have a sandwich." I attempt nonchalance. I'm impressed with Cleve's nerve. He doesn't seem the least bit afraid of Dave walking in the door.

"Dave is screwing a grad student," I say. "This isn't one-sided. I don't know what'll happen between us."

Cleve and I eat at the dining table, a battered, round-legged relic Dave and I bought and haven't got around to refinishing. Cleve tells me about a trip to California with his parents during the summer after college, about seeing the boys on the beach and deciding he would move to LA from Iowa.

He rises from his chair and goes into the bedroom, reappears in pants, shoes, and unbuttoned shirt. "Are you all right, handsome?"

"I'm fine."

"No regrets, I hope?"

"No regrets."

"I'll call you at the bookstore tomorrow. I'll be in Phoenix—it's part of my sales territory."

He's a pharmaceutical salesman, I remember after a moment.

"I should be home Thursday night," he says.

At the door I kiss him. He pulls my naked body inside his open shirt. I start to get aroused again and shove him away. I watch from behind the door as he walks to his car buttoning his shirt, climbs in, and drives off.

I find the knotted condom on the toilet tank and seal it in a letter-sized envelope I shove deep into the kitchen trash. After putting the sheets in the washer, I tuck clean sheets on the bed, shower, pull on jeans and a sweatshirt, and pace from room to room while fading daylight drains all color from the furniture and walls. In my mind, Dave's wrecked his car and is waiting for me to find him in a hospital somewhere. Ridiculous, I know.

Sitting in the dark on the living room couch, I hear the back door open. "I'm home," Dave calls. "You'll never guess what I did today." He walks into the living room swinging his briefcase and stands twirling it from one long arm. "I left half my intro biology exams on a chair in the dining commons. Drove all the way home before I knew it."

I stare up at him.

"As I opened the kitchen door, I realized my briefcase was too light and thought *Oh, shit!* I hauled ass back to campus and was so fucking relieved to see those exams still there! Can you believe it? I would have been in such deep shit! I don't think I'll give paper exams anymore."

He falls on the couch beside me, thuds his briefcase on the floor, and stretches out his legs.

I don't know whether to believe him or not.

"Are you half asleep, Len? Why are you sitting in the dark?" He reaches up and switches on the black standing lamp.

"Don't you teach on Monday afternoons?"

"Duh?" he says. "It's spring break, remember? I went to work out and thought maybe I'd get more grading done in my office than at home. I ran into Brian from engineering. He's fielding a ball team for this summer and wants me to play. I said I'd think about it."

"I forgot you're on spring break."

He glances at the kitchen. "What do you want to do about dinner?" When I don't answer, he pokes me in the ribs. "Wake up. Were you napping?"

"I guess."

"You guess?" He laughs. "You don't know whether you were napping?"

"I was reading. I fell asleep."

"Get your shoes. Let's walk down to the corner. I'm hungry."

All I can do is stare at him.

"Len, did you smoke a joint? You're *out of it*! Go splash water on your face—that'll wake you up. I've only eaten a yogurt since noon."

❖

As I turn down the bed, Dave wanders from the bathroom in his underwear, his toothbrush frothing his mouth. He glances at rose-colored sheets under our green comforter. "Clean sheets—nice." He turns and wanders back to the bathroom. I'm calm enough by now to realize Dave could have fucked Ian in his office this afternoon. But he didn't, I can tell. Even if he had, what I did feels worse because it was vengeful. I wanted Cleve, but I also wanted to cheat on Dave behind his back, a willful act. Dave fucks Ian because Dave can't help himself. Otherwise, he wouldn't jeopardize his career by screwing a student.

In bed, Dave falls asleep but I can't. I think of Cleve's cream in a condom sealed in an envelope in our kitchen trash. I slip from under the covers, pull on my jeans, and tiptoe to the kitchen. I tighten a twist tie around the plastic bag and carry it out to the cans beside the garage. A dog barks, shrill in the night, as I walk back to the house. Stopping along the cement path, I look up at the gray sky, look around at treetops jutting above the low house roofs—palm trees, pines, Italian spruce, jacarandas, acacias, a maple, an oak. I remember my first day in California, staring out from Dave's second-floor apartment wondering why California looked so different from anywhere else I'd been. Then I realized I'd never been anywhere with so many types of trees.

❖

Cleve calls the bookstore while I'm doing the morning coffee run. I gave him my store number and explained Jane insists everyone turn off their cells while at work. I didn't tell him we ignore Jane's rule when she's not here. He calls again while I'm with Jane at her accountant's office.

When Cleve and I talk, he invites me to spend the weekend at Big Bear Lake with him and some friends. "My housemate, Don, owns a place he rents to skiers most weekends. We could drive up before traffic gets bad Friday, if you can get off early."

"I can't go away for a weekend."

"Why? Dave does whatever he wants, doesn't he?"

"He hasn't gone away for a weekend."

"From what you've told me, he's not in a position to make up the rules."

I watch Ian walk behind the counter. He trades places with Rosie on the stool by the register.

"I have a conference call coming in, Lenny. Think about Big Bear, will you? I'll try to reach you tomorrow, but I have a wild day over here. I always plan too much when I'm in Phoenix." I forgot he was out of town. "If we don't talk, I'll call as soon as I'm back."

"All right."

"You have no idea how much you mean to me," he says, and he hangs up.

❖

I half listen to unflattering stories Jane's told me several times about her daughters-in-law. I'm curious how far she'll go in denigrating them. As she works her way around to telling me for the thousandth time that her younger son, Randall, is my age and makes a six-figure salary, I force an exaggerated yawn. She's unfazed.

"I just wish Ran hadn't married beneath himself," she says, "or that his poor Becky were better equipped to rise to her good fortune. I'm so anxious to see Ran's time-share in Aspen. Which reminds me, I need to ask Ian to stay at my place while I'm away. It's so inconvenient with him never here during the day. I don't know if you thought of that when you switched his hours?"

"Leave a note on his time card. I'm going to lunch."

I hope she'll be gone when I come back from my workout.

Tony isn't at the gym. I haven't seen his tattooed, dimpled buns since I called him an asshole.

Eating a roast beef sandwich happily alone at my desk, I see Ian's beautiful buns in my mind's eye. I'd love to cup them underwater in Jane's pool again. I'm aroused most of the afternoon thinking about it.

Ian saunters in, yawning, the five o'clock sun gilding the parking lot behind his long-sleeved white T-shirt and clean faded jeans. Rosie works in our small Spanish language section. I'm at the register. A woman digs through her purse looking for her credit card. I watch Ian's bare feet in black thongs as he goes into the stockroom. The woman keeps digging. I picture Ian climbing out of Jane's pool and padding around the deck to get his clothes, his bruise-colored cock sticking out like a pistol. My customer finds the card she wants and inserts it. Ian emerges from the storeroom, and he joins me at the register. I thank my woman, and she walks away with a half dozen magazines and a children's book in a plastic sack with our Royal Books logo. I let Ian take over the register. "By the way, Jane's planning to call and ask you to house-sit again."

"Where's she going?"

"Aspen."

He rolls his eyes. "Tough life. I thought this place is always on the verge of bankruptcy?"

His hair smells lemony. I want to stick my nose in his bangs, but instead I mosey into my office and sit scrolling through a book catalog while I picture him naked.

I have one hand in my pocket to hide my erection as I lock my office door for the day. Ian, alone at the counter, sits on the stool. I walk up beside him, close enough to mumble in his ear. "This afternoon I was thinking about you and me in Jane's pool."

He stares ahead impassively while I pat the blond

countertop a few times. "I'm on my way out. Have a good night."

As I hustle to the door and wave to Rosie, Ian hollers to me. I stop by the gift books table. "Would you watch the register a minute, Rosie?" Ian calls.

While she takes his place, I pick up a large volume about English gardens, as though it caught my eye in passing. Ian heads for the stockroom, glancing my way, and stops at the metal swinging door, out of Rosie's sight. He stares at me until I take a step in his direction. I keep my eye on Rosie, who is bent over, looking for something on the shelf under the counter.

Ian pushes backward through the swinging door and holds it open while I pass through. He steps into the john. I lay the English gardens book on a stack of boxes and follow. Under the bright bathroom ceiling light, we kiss and help each other out of our shirts, undo each other's pants.

"Lenny?" Rosie calls.

Ian yanks away and stuffs his boner into his jeans.

We hear the stockroom door squawking back and forth on its hinges.

"Sorry, sir. I guess he left," Rosie says, at a greater distance, while Ian pulls on his shirt, and I tuck myself into my pants. I force a quick kiss on him and tell him to go out first. "Distract Rosie so I can sneak by."

He opens the bathroom door just wide enough to squeeze through. I slip on my shirt and wait a few minutes, creep out, and cross the stockroom, brushing through the metal door without letting it swing. Ian talks to Rosie behind the counter, her back to me. I hustle to the front windows, aglow with pinkish gold sky. I figure I'll go to Winchell's and buy coffees for Ian, Rosie, and me. I want to be near him.

"Lenny," a male voice shouts. I glance sideways. Cleve smiles at me from the gift books tables.

"*Querido*, I thought you'd gone home," Rosie hollers. "That gentleman wants to speak to you."

Cleve walks toward me. In charcoal trousers, white shirt, and loosened tie, he could be a husky model in an over-thirty menswear catalog.

"I thought you were in Phoenix, Cleve?"

"I got off the plane and figured I could catch you here before you went home. Why? Is this a bad time?"

I motion for him to follow and hurry outside. The strip mall's busiest at rush hour, people running errands after work, cars crisscrossing the lot and casting long shadows in the low sun. I walk several yards to my car and spin around. Cleve almost bumps into me. "Why'd you drive all the way up here from the airport?" I say.

"I thought you'd be glad to see me."

"I don't like surprises. Not with things the way they are."

"I'm sorry."

"I have to go home."

"Can't we talk a minute somewhere? Lenny, *please*. I'll know to call first next time. I'm here now. Just a fast drink, maybe in that bar?"

He nods at the Tap Room, and I stare across the parking lot at its mock leather door.

"I didn't get a chance to call you yesterday, so when I got off the plane…"

"Okay, come on."

Indoors, in the glow of illuminated liquor ads, we climb on stools. He orders a beer, and I order a double bourbon, neat. The TV news plays, and the divorced men drink beers or whiskeys and eat sandwiches. Two business-dressed women, angled to each other on their stools, hold glasses of white wine and chat, attracting shy glances from the silent men.

I down my bourbon and stare up at the TV screen while I wait for another. With my second stubby glass in hand, I look over at Cleve. "So, how was Phoenix?"

"Routine. I go to Arizona every month."

"What do you do over there?"

"Call on accounts, the same as I do here."

He stares into his half-empty pilsner glass, tilted in his hand. I toss back my second bourbon. Turning sideways on my stool, I wrap the toe of my desert boot behind Cleve's ankle. He sits more erect, raises his beer glass and sips. "Sorry I snapped at you, Cleve."

"This hasn't turned out the way I intended."

"It's turned out okay."

"I should let you get home," he says. "I haven't been home for three days myself. Let me pay for our drinks, and we'll get out of here." He signals the bartender and pushes away my proffered money.

As we step out to a garnet sky over the parking lot, I feel euphoric from so much booze on an empty stomach. I ask where his car is.

"Beside the bookstore."

He motions, and we walk over. Parked cars cluster near the restaurant on the corner. Only Cleve's car is nosed up against the beige stucco side wall of Royal Books. I stop on the passenger side as I hear the doors unlock. "Maybe I'll get in a minute, Cleve?"

He walks around to the driver's side. The new car odor reminds me of opening the door to throw up on the gas station cement. But the luxury of Cleve's car appeals to me this evening. "You drove all the way up here to see me. I'm impressed."

"I'd drive a lot farther to see you."

I lean over and slip my hand between his legs. "I hope you don't mind the bourbon on my breath."

"I like the bourbon on your breath. I like everything about you."

I want to kiss him, but too many people can see us. "Let's go to your place, Cleve. I'll follow you in my car."

"Ride with me, and I'll bring you back. I'd rather have more time together."

"Damn, you're a nice man."

He starts the engine, and we fasten our seat belts. "I need to make a call," I say, pulling my cell out of my pants pocket.

"Tell him you'll see him tomorrow."

I smile. "You don't like Dave, do you?"

"I don't want to be his pal."

I turn away from Cleve to the passenger's window and press Dave's name on my phone. His message center picks up. "Dave, it's me. I'm—"

"I'm here." He munches on something.

I talk fast and try to sound casual. "The new gal I hired, Honey, is sick, and she's scheduled to work with Ian, so I need to stay. What are you eating?"

"A carrot. I'm writing the paper I'll give in Chicago next month. I'll keep working."

"There's stuff for dinner in the refrigerator."

"I'm taking a chicken pie out of the freezer as we speak."

"I should go. I have a customer waiting."

"See you when you get here."

I press End and wonder if I should ask Cleve to take me back to my car. I could go home, tell Dave that Rosie showed up for Honey, so I didn't have to stay. No harm done.

❖

Cleve lives just off Balboa Boulevard, on a short block leading to the beach. A garage door opens below the house, set close to the street, and we pull in. Cleve gets his suitcase out of the trunk. As we climb exterior pebble-surfaced stairs without risers, I hear and smell the ocean at a distance in the dark.

He unlocks a door and motions me into a cocoa-carpeted living room, where a leather sofa makes an L around a coffee table of boomerang-shaped glass on driftwood. An older man, bald and pregnant looking, perches on a rattan stool at a bar between the living room and kitchen. Peering over half-lensed glasses, he scans me from head to toe and chuckles.

"Ah, *yes*. You must be Lenny. I'm Don."

He holds out a fleshy pink hand, and I take a few steps and shake it. He wears a light blue cardigan with dark blue trousers and moccasins, his bare ankles as fleshy pink as his hands. On the bar a bottle of sparkling water keeps company with a skillet of nuts on a dish towel. Don's tongue flicks at his teeth and lips, cleaning. His breath smells of nuts. I try to imagine him and Cleve as lovers twenty years ago.

Eyes twinkling, Don motions at the skillet. "Do you want some hot nuts?"

"Thanks, I'm saving my appetite." I wink.

Cleve smiles and slips an arm around my waist. "Let me show you the balcony." He ushers me out through a sliding glass door. "In daylight, you can see the ocean to the left."

I see the alley-width street end at a cement boardwalk with streetlamps. Sand disappears into darkness beyond the walk. Two college-age guys in swim trunks smoke a joint on a lighted balcony across the narrow road. I can make out their small erect nipples.

"We'll take a walk on the beach later," Cleve says. "Why don't I go make drinks? What would you like?"

"To be in your bed."

Squeezing my hand, he leads me indoors. Don is gone from his perch at the bar. I hear a TV elsewhere in the house.

Cleve's bedroom is large and thickly carpeted, like the living room, only in dark green. A king-sized bed floats just above the floor, with a low bookcase headboard lit by mini-spot lamps. A knotty pine bookcase fills a side wall.

We undress apart, watching each other. We wrestle on a firm mattress with taut gray flannel sheets, testing each other's strength. I start a dialogue of quiet profanity, like a porn script, until he pins me and kisses me.

"Make me suck your cock," I say.

He straddles my chest, and I tongue the secreting hole of his cock. I wrap my lips around it. I relax my throat and ingest the full length of his fat shaft till his balls press my chin. He pulls his cock out and licks his way down my chest, takes me in his mouth. He lets me go and leans over me, to reach the headboard for KY and a condom. He raises my legs and places the rubber in my hand. While I roll it on him, he sucks my big toe.

His thrusts are slow and firm. He looks into my eyes the whole while. "I'm about to come, Lenny. I can't hold it back any longer. I love you. I want you to know it." He spasms. I pull him down and bury my face in his neck and rub my cock and balls against his belly till I come in his chest hair, matted between us.

Smiling, only fingertips touching on the wide bed, we lie on our stomachs cooling off. I start laughing. "I gave you a hickey, Cleve."

He feels a bump on his neck and smiles.

He gets up, walks through a doorway, and switches on a bathroom light. Over the sound of the exhaust fan, I hear water running in a sink. I fold my hands beneath my head and lie staring at the ceiling. I try to imagine living in this room with

Cleve. I try to picture myself living anywhere with someone other than Dave. I think of Dave going off to Baltimore with Ian and feel an earthquake in my guts.

Cleve comes out of the bathroom in a white terrycloth robe, kisses me, and drops a matching robe on the mattress near me. "I'll put some chicken breasts in the oven. Take a nap if you like."

I rise on my elbows and look around for a clock. "What time is it, Cleve?"

He looks past me, to the headboard. "Not quite nine."

"I can't stay much longer."

"Why?"

"I just can't." I scoot off the bed. "Could I take a quick shower?"

"Go ahead." His voice is troubled.

In a dark maroon bathroom with a black counter and a black tub, I shower and rinse my mouth with Listerine. I dress and head into the living room, where Cleve, still in his robe, sits on the sofa.

"Can we go?"

"You're not even staying for dinner? What are you worried about? Your boyfriend goes out, doesn't he?"

"I have to go, Cleve."

He gets up from the couch, disappears into the bedroom, and returns in a zipped gray sweatshirt, jeans, and sandals. He switches off the oven and the burner under a pan. I step outside to the landing, and he follows. I look for the college boys across the way, but they've gone. The garage door rolls up noisily as we descend the stairs.

We ride along residential Balboa Boulevard without talking. "You have a nice house," I say as we roll onto busier, commercial Newport Boulevard, toward the freeway.

He doesn't reply until I glance over.

"The house is Don's. He bought it a few years back. Another friend was planning to move in but changed his mind, so I did. I love living at the beach. We could have gone for a walk after dinner."

I press my head to the back of the seat and watch the rear of a Porsche in front of us.

Cleve glances at me while we sit at a red light. "I guess coming up to Big Bear this weekend is out of the question?"

I forgot he invited me to Big Bear when he phoned from Phoenix. "I'm afraid so."

"I don't understand why. Your boyfriend, or whatever he is, is seeing someone. You can see someone."

We ride several blocks without talking. Flowing onto the freeway, Cleve starts music, something classical I don't recognize. I listen and gaze at three lanes of taillights moving steadily at seventy miles an hour, mesmerizing. "I like the music. What is it?"

"Rodrigo. *Concierto de Aranjuez.*"

I ask if we can hear it again. He restarts it.

We roll up and over the elevated sweep of curve from the Costa Mesa Freeway to the Riverside. I like riding on Southern California freeways at night, the feeling of being in an enclosed bubble surrounded by other bubbles passing thousands of houses and stores, with palm trees jutting up into the night sky.

Cleve clears his throat. "I haven't fallen for anyone in a long time. I suppose maybe it's not healthy for me."

"Only you know that, Cleve. I won't lead you on. I love Dave. I was faithful to him for almost four years. Before that, we broke up because I fucked other guys. The guy he's fucking now works for me at the bookstore, and I have a boner for him, too, so I understand Dave's infatuation. If Dave leaves me for Ian, or I get tired of waiting for them to get over each other, maybe I'll be ready to fall for you. But maybe you won't want me then. Sometimes attraction works that way. I've seen it. Or maybe we'd both find out I'm not an easy dog to keep on the porch. I can't make promises about the future, Cleve."

He reaches over and strokes my inner leg. "You're the most important thing in my life right now, Lenny."

We pull off the freeway on to Harbor Boulevard, near the bookstore. He turns into the parking lot and stops next to my car, facing the neon sign of the Tap Room across the lot.

"I'll call you?"

"If you want to." After sitting quietly a moment, I say, "Have fun at Big Bear this weekend. Don't do anything I wouldn't do." I grin and hop out of his car and into mine.

❖

Dave hears me and wanders into the kitchen. "You had a long day."

"I'm hungry." I slide a can of chili out of an overhead cabinet. "I meant to order a pizza, but the store got busy."

He pecks me on the lips.

Avoiding his eyes, I open the can and dump its contents into a saucepan. I should come clean about Cleve, but I'm terrified of making it easier for Dave to leave me.

"My paper's taking shape," he says.

"Good." I yawn despite being nervous. "I'm tired."

"While you're eating, I'll go finish a thought." He heads back to his den.

I eat my chili.

In bed, he falls asleep while I listen to cars pass on Brookhurst and think about Michael. Today is the second anniversary of his death. I try to remember the last time Michael and I made love. We let our relationship cool the summer after high school because we knew I would be going off to Haverford College, in Pennsylvania. I remember being in my room when my mom came home from shopping and yelled up the stairs that Galveston was under a tornado warning. Michael and I hadn't noticed the early afternoon getting dark. Was that the last time we made love? Whatever was the last, we didn't realize it. How can two people do something so important without knowing it?

We were friends—sisters, Michael said—when I came home for Thanksgiving during that first year of college.

I ease out of bed and tiptoe into Dave's den, pull the door closed, and switch on his desk lamp. Under a stack of printed-out articles, I find the page with the Baltimore job ads on it. Staring at the sheet as though it's a legal document—a death certificate, a divorce decree—I carefully fold it a few times, carry it into the bedroom, and stuff it into my wallet.

❖

The bookstore's busy with a Brownie troop as Ian arrives to take over the register from Rosie. I nod from my desk and try to give him a meaningful look, although I don't know what meaning I intend. So he won't think I want to blow him in the john, I leave him alone and continue sending Royal Books' social media followers messages about new titles and some vintage books I figure might be unheard of to younger readers. Most people who see my messages and want a book order it from an online megastore. Many people who come through our door use us as a showroom and order books online.

Glancing up from my screen, I see the Brownie troop has left and Rosie's gone. I also see Melinda standing across the counter from Ian. I've never seen her in the store before. I decide to mosey out and say hello.

Watching me approach, Melinda straightens up from leaning on the counter, gathers her long chestnut hair, and tucks it behind her ears. She wears the pink sweater she wore at Jane's house the afternoon she caught Ian and me in the pool.

"I haven't seen you for a while, Melinda."

"Hi, there." She smiles. Her eyes return to Ian. "Anyhow, you're invited. Susan's cooking."

"God, I'll meet your mother!"

"I'm afraid you will."

The phone rings, and Ian answers it. "Just a minute, please," he says, handing me the receiver.

"Lenny Anders. May I help you?"

"Hi, handsome."

"Cleve," I mumble, "why aren't you on your way to Big Bear?"

"I'm *at* Big Bear. I wondered if we could make plans for dinner Monday?"

"I don't know. I can't talk now."

Cleve's silent.

"Call me when you're back, okay? We're in the middle of a rush here. Have a good weekend, Cleve." I hang up.

"A *rush?*" Ian says. "What was that about?"

"Nothing. I wasn't in the mood to gab. Send calls to my office instead of shoving the phone at me."

"You were standing beside me, *boss*. Your line wouldn't ring out here unless you switched it over."

"I know. My fault."

"You could have gone into your office, and I would've switched the call back."

"I didn't want to talk. Forget it."

Melinda's bright eyes scrutinize me.

"I'm heading home," I say. I tell her and Ian to have a good weekend.

Outside the store, I glance back and see her leaning across the counter again, close to him. I wonder if she's saying something about me.

❖

"You could return my calls," Cleve says. He leans back against a blue van parked near the storefront. He wears a white T-shirt and gray sweats in which the head of his dick shows like a pool ball.

"The store's been busy all day," I say, as though that's why I haven't phoned him back. It's Tuesday afternoon. Cleve called twice yesterday and once this morning.

"Bullshit, Lenny. If you don't want to see me anymore, at least pick up the phone and say so."

"I don't know what I want."

"You won't get less confused by hiding."

"I was planning to call you. You're not wearing a suit today."

"I gave myself a day off."

"How was your weekend at Big Bear?"

He ignores my question. He's unshaven, and his brushed-back black hair looks wild. He pushes his sunglasses up on his forehead, above bloodshot eyes.

"Dave stopped seeing the guy he was fucking," I lie.

"Does that mean you have to stop seeing me?"

Glancing around the parking lot, I watch a pickup drive toward us, sun glinting off its windshield.

"Lenny, come to my place Saturday. Take a walk on the beach with me. I'll be in New Zealand for three weeks after that."

"You travel a lot."

"Not really. I haven't taken an actual vacation for years. Say you'll come Saturday. We don't have to go to bed."

"That sounds like 'I won't come in your mouth.' Not that I've ever minded anyone coming in my mouth. Although with AIDS, a person has to be careful."

"Are you worried about AIDS? Is that it? I was tested a year ago, and I haven't done anything unsafe since."

A man startles us by striding up to the van Cleve leans against, and he and I step away from it.

"I should get back to work, Cleve. I'll see you Saturday. What time?"

"You're not just saying you'll come?"

"No. I want to."

"One o'clock? So we'll have the afternoon? I'll make something for lunch. Cooking's a hobby of mine. We can eat on the balcony and hear the ocean."

"Cool."

I walk him to his car and stand with my hands in my pockets while he climbs in. As he starts to roll away, I shout, "Wait a minute." Walking around to the passenger's side, I climb in. "Go out the driveway across the parking lot from the doughnut shop." I point. "Then drive straight across Harbor Boulevard and into the neighborhood."

"Where are we going?"

"Nowhere. You'll see."

While we circle side streets in a neighborhood in which some houses are stucco, others cement block, some well-kept, others not so much so, I undo Cleve's sweatpants and take his cock in my mouth. In only a few heartbeats, I taste his cum.

When I sit back up, he looks like he doesn't know what happened to him. "That's not why I drove up here," he says.

"I know."

"I want a life together, Lenny."

"Let's start with a walk on the beach."

He drops me in front of the bookstore. As he pulls away, I linger outside watching patches of fog float across the otherwise sunny parking lot like sails over a lake. When the fog is so thick I can barely see the strip mall fifty yards away, I turn and step indoors.

❖

At noon Saturday I still haven't told Dave I'm going out for a while. We took a long run, showered, and cooked eggs and waffles we're eating at the table in our dining area. Dave gets up to pour more milk. His phone, lying on the kitchen counter, plays bars of the *William Tell* Overture. He answers and listens more than he talks, then he leans through the doorway. "Ian wants to know if we'd like to drive down to the beach when he gets off work."

I stare at Dave with his cell to his ear. He lowers it and holds his thumb over the microphone. "I can tell him no, Len. I have a lot of stuff I could get done today."

"Tell him yes."

"Lenny's up for it. We'll pick you up at the store at three?"

While I mop a forkful of waffle in syrup, I listen to Dave say "Sure" a few times.

We finish eating and carry our plates to the dishwasher. I consider how I can call Cleve without Dave knowing it. Dave brings his computer and a tax folder from his den and spreads out statements and receipts on the dining table. I did my taxes at work, when Jane wasn't there. Mine are simple. I make piss little and have no deductions. While Dave organizes his mess, I get my wallet and phone from the bedroom. "I'll walk down to the market for orange juice, so we'll have it in the morning," I say.

Before I get to the front door in my flip-flops, Dave pops up from his chair. "I'll come along. I don't feel like doing my taxes now."

When we return with the orange juice, I consider slipping out into the backyard to call Cleve, but Dave might see me and ask who I was talking to. Instead, I lock myself in the bathroom and send Cleve a text message.

In midafternoon Ian waits out front of the bookstore in a tan T-shirt, jeans, and tennis shoes. His smooth blue-black hair gives off sparks of sunlight. I jump out and hold open the car door, smiling at him as he scrambles into the back seat. I'm so anxious to call Cleve I could wet my pants. Leaning down, I look across to Dave behind the steering wheel. "I want to check something in my office—I'll be two minutes."

I wave to Rosie and Honey as I rush across the store. Sitting at my desk, I lean over an open lower file drawer in the wild chance Dave and Ian could see me on the phone from the car. I dial Cleve and listen to his recorded message. At the tone, I talk. "Cleve, it's Lenny. Are you there? Something came up and I couldn't make it today. Sorry I couldn't call you earlier. I hope you got my text message." I was due at his place two hours ago. "Cleve? Okay, I'll try to reach you later."

❖

In cool afternoon sun, Dave, Ian, and I sit on a yacht-sized outcrop of rock at the base of a cliff along Laguna Beach. Whitecaps splash over formations farther out. The tide leaves pools in our outcrop's bowls and crevices. People clamber over our fortress to get from one arc of sand to the next. We talk about our respective college years, about cars we like, about Dave's nephew in suburban Chicago, recently caught cutting class to make out in the high school parking lot, according to Dave's sister.

We sit quietly as the sun congeals into an orange ball and drops into the ocean, leaving the sky dusty pink.

In twilight, we climb two flights of wood steps wedged into the cliff and follow a short side street uphill to the Coast Highway. Across the highway, we crowd into a noisy seafood restaurant with a pizza parlor ambience. We wait for our table at a rosined wooden bar, bottles of beer in our hands.

Carrying our second beers, we scoot into a booth. A chalkboard on the wall lists the menu. Dave studies it and looks across the table to Ian. "We used to drive up to Baltimore and eat seafood in an old waterfront neighborhood."

"I keep trying to picture Baltimore."

"We have some snapshots we took there," Dave says. "I don't know how much of the city they show, but we can dig them out if we go back to the house."

A smiling blond college-aged waitress takes our orders. She asks if anyone would like another beer. Dave and Ian say no. I've chugged most of my second and want to say yes, but I feel Dave's eyes on the side of my head.

"A Coke, please."

Our waitress hurries away, and I slide out of our booth and stand up. "We went to a German restaurant in Baltimore for my birthday one year," I tell Ian. "Maybe you guys can go there sometime." I glance around to assess which direction will lead me to the bathroom. "I have to piss."

I walk carefully, afraid I might appear tipsy after two beers on an empty stomach. The men's room has a urinal and a toilet, someone peeing at each. I wait my turn. I wash my hands and squeeze out the door, politely smiling at an inbound older man in a checkered shirt. I walk through the bar, past the hostess at the front of the restaurant, and out the door.

Traffic pokes along Coast Highway, a solid parade of headlights and taillamps. I smell the ocean, feel it on my skin in the cool night air. I come to our car, the red sport coupe Dave drives. I wasn't looking for it. I stop and stare at its profile, reflecting light from a shop window. I could get in, drive off, and leave Dave and Ian stranded.

Cutting across the street, I flip off a driver who honks at me. I trot down a sloping side road to the cliff above the ocean and descend two flights of steps. A stretch of beach curves ahead of me. Walking just below the high tide line on the firm, damp sand, I start around the gentle arc. The ocean and seaward sky are black, like a cavern. Only a few pale stars, small as salt granules, give evidence of vastness. Swells of white foam, luminous in the ambient shore light, accompany roars of surf.

To my landward side, multistory houses drop down the cliff, their gated stairways extending to the sand. Most of the houses are dark, except for security lights.

Jane's younger son, a patent attorney, has a house overlooking the ocean in Santa Barbara. Both of Jane's sons inherited money from their father's parents. More money than I'll ever see.

If Dave leaves me, I won't be able to keep our house. If Dave leaves me, I won't *want* our house. Maybe I'll go stay with my mom in Galveston, look for a job and an apartment in Houston. I'm still in touch with friends of Michael there.

I like Cleve. I'll never see him again. I remember how I felt about being jerked around by guys I was dating.

Water splashes the side of my sneaker, and I move higher

on the sand. I'm near the end of the arc. Ahead, the cliff bulges out into the sea.

I turn and walk in the direction I came from. I wonder what Dave and Ian thought when I didn't come back to the table. I feel foolish.

At the steps I came down, I climb up and follow the sloping side street.

Dave and Ian stand on the sidewalk on the opposite side of Coast Highway. Their butts lean against our low coupe, their backs to me as I cross the road and walk behind the car to join them. Dave sees me and stands up.

"There you are." His voice is cautious, upbeat. A white sack sits on the car hood—the shrimp and French fries I ordered, I assume. Ian straightens up, gives me a friendly embarrassed glance, and turns to stare at dresses in a shop window. Dave squeezes my shoulder. "We wondered where you went."

"My stomach got queasy all of a sudden. I needed some air. Ready to go?"

"Sure."

Dave picks up the white sack from the hood as he walks around to the driver's side. I hold the passenger's door open while Ian clambers into the back seat. Pulling out of the parking space, Dave lays his hand on my thigh. "Are you feeling better?"

"Walking helped. How was the food?"

"Not great."

While we edge past shops and restaurants in the traffic of the small downtown, he and Ian elaborate about what they ate.

"Maybe we shouldn't be talking about food?" Dave says.

"I'm fine now."

We turn into Laguna Canyon for the drive through the hills. Dave starts music, modern rock.

"I want to go to Ireland once I sell my house," Ian says, from the back seat.

Dave tells him about our trip to Europe the summer before last and brags about my French until he coaxes me to say how much I liked Paris. I'm too humiliated to say more.

We flow onto the San Diego Freeway. As we ride up it and merge with the Santa Ana, I listen to Dave's travelogue, appreciating his reliable savoir-faire. Whenever he falters, Ian asks a question. Dave drives with both hands on the wheel, but one hand occasionally leaves it to knead my thigh. I sit as still as a stone.

"Remember my car is at the bookstore," Ian says as we approach the Harbor Boulevard exit.

"We can take you to your car in the morning," I say.

Dave glances over at me. Ian's silent.

"Shouldn't we drop Ian at his car, Len? If you're not feeling so good?"

"I'm okay."

We pass the Harbor Boulevard exit. Dave glances in the rearview mirror. "I wouldn't go back to the restaurant we ate at."

"I wouldn't either," Ian says. "My swordfish was too buttery."

"So was my grouper."

They're both nervous. They want to have sex as much as I do. They want it with each other, maybe with me.

At the house, I hurry ahead of them, go straight into the guest room, and open out the sofa bed. I fit the flimsy mattress with our only queen-sized sheets.

Dave and Ian make coffee. When I join them, I see the sack holding my dinner on the counter. I put it in the refrigerator so it wouldn't remind me I actually walked out of a restaurant.

Taking Ian in my arms, I'm surprised by his responsiveness.

On the sofa bed, I'm conscious only of Ian's body. He and I are an object floating in space. I don't mind Dave being in the room, on the bed. I even tell Dave to fuck me while I'm fucking Ian. The feel of Dave's finger in my ass becomes a part of the feeling of Ian's body.

Naked and chilly, I eat my leftover dinner at our dining table. I eat fast, without talking. The plastic tray full of shrimp and French fries still shames me.

Dave and Ian—also chilly, judging by the nubs of their nipples sticking out—eat sandwiches. We drink beers Dave opened. I'm planning what we'll do when we get back into bed. I want to have my two lovers kneel by my face, one on each side, while I stroke them off.

And I do. I fall asleep on my back, with their cream drying on my nose and cheeks and forehead and in my hair.

Waking at daybreak, I realize only Dave is in bed. I stumble to my feet and look for Ian's clothes on the floor. Dave stirs on the mattress and lifts his mouth from the pillow. "I drove Ian to the bookstore to get his car last night." Dave's voice is hoarse from sleep. "A painter is working on his house this morning. Come back to bed, Len."

The guest room is thick with our odors as I crawl back on to the mattress.

"That's better," Dave murmurs, folding his long arm over me before he falls back to sleep.

5. PEARLS

Dave calls me at the bookstore, his voice circumspect. He had lunch with Ian, and Ian asked what we were doing tonight. We seldom do anything on weekdays.

"I don't know, Dave. What *are* we doing?"

"Do you want him to come over when he gets off work?"

"If he wants to."

"You'll see him at five, Len. If you want him to come over, tell him. I have to go. It's time for my class."

After we hang up, Rosie leans through my office doorway and asks how Dave is. She transferred his call to me.

"Fine. How's Mussolini?"

"*Querido*, I need to talk to you about him." She bites her lip.

I've met Mussolini, whose real name is Alan Smith. He's skinny and not as handsome a man as Rosie deserves, although he's sexy in an arrogant intellectual way, like another guy she dated.

"Alan was awarded a grant to spend a year in Italy, and I've decided to go with him."

"Wow! This is serious. You're leaving me!"

She nods and smiles, her eyes filling with tears. I rise from my chair and put my arms around her, blinking back my own tears.

"How sweet, *querido*. All this time we thought we just lusted after each other's bodies, and now we find out we like each other, too."

"I'll miss you, Rosie."

"I won't be leaving until sometime in June. I'll give notice as soon as I can."

"I don't even want to think about it."

❖

In the literature alcove, I'm perusing the middle of *Washington Square*, a book I've read almost as many times as the children's books I wore out as a kid. I catch sight of Jane's yellow head coming in the front door. I'm surprised because it's almost five. I figured she wouldn't show up today. She doesn't see me. I shove *Washington Square* back on the shelf and watch her carry a clothing store bag into our office.

I cross the floor slowly. Jane stands behind her desk rubbing lotion on her hands and staring at my note saying her dentist needs to reschedule an appointment. I don't know why his office called the store. After wiping her hands on a Kleenex, she pulls a large white box out of the bag and takes off its lid.

I stop in our office doorway. "I have bad news, Jane—Rosie's leaving."

Jane lifts from the box the bodice and sleeves of a pale green dress. She caresses the material with her long-nailed, bony fingers.

"Rosie's leaving," I repeat, stepping into the office and standing behind my chair.

Jane's eyes remain fixed on her dress. "Surely you're not worried about replacing Rosita. A twit like Honey would be an improvement."

Obviously, Honey's honeymoon is over.

"Since we may be replacing Ian, too," Jane says, "let's both interview all applicants, please."

She raises the shoulders of the dress higher and lifts it away from her desk so the skirt hangs free from the box.

I grab my jacket off the hook behind the door and escape before I say something I won't be able to take back.

"Am I seeing you guys later?" Ian says as I start around the service counter.

I stop and face him. "I forgot Dave mentioned it."

"I don't have to come over. Whatever you want."

"Sure, come over."

He'd like more encouragement, but I turn and hustle out to the parking lot.

❖

During dinner, Dave doesn't ask whether Ian's coming. Afterward, I lie on the living room sofa with my phone and update my half-assed online presence. Bored with that, I pick up from the floor a men's magazine I like for the hot guys and for the occasional article about one of them doing something über manly, like risking his life to save others. Dave leans out through his den doorway. "Ten minutes, Len."

"It isn't on tonight." A detective miniseries we watch. "Something's on in its place."

"Something good?"

"I don't remember. Look for yourself if you want to know." I snap to the next page in my magazine. Dave lingers in his doorway fiddling with the zipper of a black sweatshirt he's wearing with jeans.

"Did you tell Ian to drop by?" he says.

"Why not?"

Stepping into the living room, Dave bends over and picks up a sports magazine lying on the floor. I bought it because of a diver in a skimpy Speedo on the cover. Dave flips the magazine open. "You don't seem to be in a good mood."

"Fuck you, Dave."

"What'd you say?"

"You heard me."

"I didn't think we talked that way to each other."

He stares down at me while I raise my magazine in front of my face. Flipping back to where I was reading before I snapped a page ahead, I scan a few more sentences about barefoot running, then slap the magazine on the floor beside *One Hundred Years of Solitude,* which I'm rereading. I pick it up and open to my bookmark. I lose concentration every time Dave rustles a magazine page in his den.

He pads into the kitchen, and I hear him open and close the refrigerator and the microwave. Glancing through the doorway, I see a ripped frozen pizza box on the counter.

He catches me looking. "Maybe having Ian over tonight isn't a good idea?" he says. "I can tell him we're tired, if you want."

"That's why you're making a pizza for him?"

My question is punctuated by a rap on the front door.

"Open the damn door, Dave."

He walks past my feet sticking over the couch arm. I don't look to watch him open the front door but hear the sound, like something coming unglued, and then hear Ian mumble as he steps inside.

I act like I'm reading. I'm wearing shorts and a long-sleeved yellow T-shirt that fits like skin. I think I'm lying perfectly still until I hear my toes crack. Over the top of my book, I watch Ian nod to me and follow Dave into the kitchen. They move away from the doorway. I can't see them. I read a page over several times without knowing what it says.

The house begins to smell of pizza. The microwave *bings*. I get up from the couch and carry my book to the kitchen doorway. Dave's back is more to me than not, his sweatshirt hanging loose, unzipped. Ian faces him, obviously fingering Dave's nipples. Ian doesn't stop when he sees me.

"The pizza's done," I say, opening the microwave.

Ian walks out of the kitchen. In a moment we hear him pissing. Dave lays his hand on my arm, and I knock it off. "What was that for?" he says.

I shove him, and he stumbles against the refrigerator. He straightens up and glares at me like I'm crazy. I glare back.

Returning to the kitchen, Ian looks from one of us to the other. He peels off his brown sweater and white T-shirt in one motion, and drops them to the floor. He takes off his black sneakers and white socks, drops them. He shrugs out of his jeans and briefs, and stands naked and erect under the bright kitchen ceiling light. He unzips my pants, pulls out my pulsing cock, and drops to his knees. I look down at his hair, at his lightly tanned shoulders, at his round, white buttocks, at his calf muscles, at the soles of his feet. I slip in and out of his mouth until I know that with one more thrust I'll come. Instead I lead him and Dave into our bedroom and kneel on all fours crosswise on our high double bed. I come while Ian fucks me as I blow Dave.

We return to the kitchen and eat cold pizza and drink beer as we lean against the counter, our spent, plump dicks nesting birdlike on swollen scrotums.

Dave opens out our sofa bed, and we spend the night on it. I lie between Dave and Ian, eventually listening to them sleep and wondering if I'm foolish to worry about them running off to Baltimore.

In the morning Dave showers as I kiss Ian at our front

door. A postcard blue sky makes the low stucco houses across the street look even snugger to the ground. A Santa Ana wind gusts. Sheets of newspaper kite down wide Brookhurst among the traffic. One tattered page clings to our rose bushes. I follow Ian outside in my bright red briefs, the wind chilly to my wet head. Sparrows hop about the lawn, chirping. I pick newspaper shreds out of the rose bushes while Ian walks around his car. Standing by the driver's door, he laughs at me, out front in my underpants. "Look at the mountains, Lenny," he yells. I nod. Snowcapped peaks rise behind distant green foothills beyond Brookhurst's dead end a couple of blocks away. I lean down, sniffing a rose, as Ian climbs into his car. He rolls away, blowing me a kiss.

❖

In a blue denim jacket and jeans, Ian drifts into the bookstore from the windy parking lot, the strip mall golden in the five o'clock sun. While he heads for the time clock, I wait in my office doorway, smiling, hands in my pockets to hide my erection, a mint in my mouth in case I have coffee breath.

Ian emerges from the stockroom carrying a dog-eared philosophy anthology he's been reading lately and comes behind the counter. I enjoy the sight of his bod, then savor the smell of his hair and skin as he passes as though I'm invisible. He climbs on the stool at the register. I jiggle coins and keys in my pockets. My erection wilts. "Something the matter, Ian?"

"Nope."

I mosey over to him. "You look glum."

"You sound like Rosie." She nicknamed Ian Eeyore, for the pessimistic *Winnie the Pooh* donkey.

"You don't look glad to see me," I say.

He shrugs.

"I'm glad to see you," I tell him.

"We're different people. In different orbits."

"We weren't in different orbits last night."

"We *are*," he says, opening his book. He starts reading or pretending to.

I don't understand you, I want to whine, when suddenly I think I do understand. "You're in love with Dave, so you don't want to be friends with me—is that it? You weaken at moments and regret it later?"

Stony-eyed, he stares at me.

"Sometimes you tire me out, Ian." I retreat into my office.

❖

"You sound subdued," my mom says over the phone in her Texas accent, acquired during the thirty-some years since she moved from Illinois as a newlywed.

"Subdued?"

"And a little grouchy?"

I'm quiet while she waits. I know I've been irritable with Dave all weekend. I sneeze. The kitchen's chilly. I'm sitting on the dryer. It has a load of clothes in it, but even with its warmth a shirt would feel good. I've been chilly all morning and haven't bothered to put one on. At least I'm wearing jeans instead of shorts. I tell Mom about Rosie giving notice. Mom knows how much I like Rosie. She also knows I loathe Jane. "I guess I'm feeling stuck."

"One of the teachers at my school quit and studied law when he was fifty."

"I don't want to go to law school!"

"I didn't *mean* you should go to law school, son-of-mine. Nor did I mean you should wait until you're fifty to do whatever you want to do."

We're silent for a moment.

"How's Dave?"

"Fine."

"Nothing's wrong between you fellows, I hope?"

"No." Her intuitive powers scare me. "He's in his den, up to his eyebrows in work. This is a hectic time of semester for him."

She's quiet a moment. "Well, I got three bids on rebuilding my bulkhead."

I thump my bare heels against the dryer while she talks about the bulkhead along the canal behind her house. I want her to probe deeper about Dave and me. When I was little, she got me to blab everything going on in my life, whether I wanted to or not. I don't intend to tell her Dave and I are having trouble, but I would like her to get *nearer* the truth. If he runs off with Ian, I wonder if I'll ever swallow my pride and tell her he fell in love with someone else.

"Lenny, honey, I need to get in the shower. DeeAnne Maubie and I are going to a ballet in Houston this afternoon. I'm sorry to cut our conversation short."

"Don't worry about it. Say hi to DeeAnne for me."

I hardly know DeeAnne Maubie. She and Mom volunteer as ushers for Galveston's community theater.

Hopping off the washing machine, feeling unmothered, I sneeze a couple of more times.

In Dave's den, I stand silently behind him as he reads a draft of the paper he'll give in Chicago next week. The burning, dusty scent of his high-intensity desk lamp competes with the smell of coffee in his mug. Absorbed, scratching his tank-shirted back, he doesn't know I'm here until I squeeze his shoulders. He tips his head up, and his slept-in hair tumbles softly against my sternum. He looks up at me with pale blue eyes. "How's your mom?"

"Fine." I clear my throat as I stare at him, our faces upside down to each other's. "I have a question for you, Dave. Are you going to Baltimore with Ian?"

He lowers his head, stares at the printed pages lying on his desktop. "I'm not going anywhere."

"Good." I slide my fingers from his shoulders to his arms, feel his biceps.

"I'm sorry if you worried about that, Len. Ian's going."

"He's made up his mind?"

"He says he has."

Kissing the top of Dave's head, I stare at a stream of sun crossing the dark wood floor, giving the boards the color and sheen of maple syrup. I leave Dave watching a brown spider crawl across the California map on the wall above his desk. He uses his pencil eraser to make it change directions.

For the rest of the day, we're gentle with each other, soft spoken, our eyes never quite meeting but brushing past, like the eyes of bashful strangers attracted to one another.

❖

Honey is leaning against my office door frame while I sit at my desk and hear about the business school at UC Irvine—I said I might want to get an MBA. As she talks, she winds strands of hair around her index finger and pulls them forward, under her chin. Her faint brown eyes are full of light. She wears a pale blue sweater and dark green slacks, and she smells like cotton candy.

Ian walks past behind her, nodding hello to me.

"Your relief's here, Honey," I say, glancing through my office window.

She looks over her shoulder, lets the wrapped hair spring free, and skips to the register, where she and Ian exchange words and laugh. Honey takes her book bag from under the counter and flees to the stockroom.

After Ian waits on a customer, he lays his anthology on the stool and stands leaning over the counter. I stare at his butt for a couple of minutes and then get up from my desk and saunter over to him. He straightens up.

"Dave says you've decided to go to Hopkins?"

"I guess so."

"Hopkins is a first-rate school. And Baltimore's full of gay guys."

Ian picks up his book and climbs on the stool. "Are you anxious to get rid of me, Lenny?"

"I'm not anxious to get rid of you."

He opens his book.

"Ian, if you think I won't miss you, you're way wrong. You're one of my closest friends. I hope we'll never lose touch."

He stares at me impassively.

"God, I don't know why I try to talk to you," I moan and head to the front of the store, to step out for a breath of fresh air before my last hour of work.

Two nights later—six nights after he last slept with us—Ian asks if he can come over when he gets off. "Sure, I'd love it," I say. He grins and says he wants to suck both of us off. I tell him to check his mouth for sores, and he asks if something's wrong. "No, but you should always examine your mouth for sores or bleeding gums before you suck anyone off."

"I know, *Mother*," he says.

That night in our guest room, Ian wants Dave and me on our feet. I watch him kneel and move from Dave's cock to mine, mine to Dave's, Dave's to mine. Dave and I stand at right angles to each other. I see Dave watching me, staring at my chest. The toes of my foot flex over Dave's toes. I glance down at Ian and propel myself in and out of his mouth, in and out. I look at Dave. He meets my eye and nods. He's watching me. My man is ogling my body at its manliest.

"You look good, Len," he breathes. "You look so fucking good."

"Watch me come, lover."

He does, and I wallow in his attention. I savor my cowboy's eyes drinking me up.

Dave comes in Ian's mouth after me and then stands at the foot of the sofa bed while I put Ian on his belly and make him moan and swear with my sheathed, rejuvenated cock. Dave throws off my rhythm by disappearing from the room but returns in a moment with his phone. *Dave's filming me fucking. Dave's filming my feet and my legs and my ass and my back.* The words repeat in my head like a chorus. Ian utters every profanity he knows and comes, and then I come. I kiss his neck, roll on my back, and pull Ian on top of me. Dave doesn't say anything, but his eyes tell me how good I looked fucking Ian.

At daybreak, I wake as Dave crawls out of bed. "I have to pack yet," he says. He's flying to Chicago later. I stay under the blanket and hear the shower start across the hall. I spoon against Ian and drift back to sleep. When I wake next, I don't hear the shower. I'm on my back, uncovered. The twisted sheet and blanket trail on the floor. Ian straddles my waist.

"I'm so in love with you, Lenny," he says, sitting erect, his balls nestling my belly, his stiff dick pointing up at me. In waking confusion, I glimpse Dave's damp head in the doorway, glimpse his green T-shirt with the coiled snake on front, and below the shirt his white thighs and brown bush and plump penis curved over his ball sack. He backs into the shadow of the hall. I try to make out his expression, to see whether he heard Ian.

Dave disappears, and I hear the closet door in our bedroom roll open. "I want your cream," I say to Ian as I pull his body astride me, up to my mouth. I position my pillow so my head tips back. I relax my throat and take the full length of Ian's slightly curved bone. He balls my face and says *ah, Jesus* and *Jesus Christ* over and over until he comes. As he starts to withdraw, I taste the little of his cream that didn't go straight down my esophagus. I stop him from climbing off me. I stroke my cock while I savor the fleshiness of his waning erection in my mouth, the basic fellow male appendage I hunger for. I feel the shape of each of his firm testicles pressing my chin, and I wrap my lips around one of them as I come.

I ask, afterward, if I hurt his ball.

"Hell, no. I love you kissing my balls."

"Our boy's becoming a man," I say.

He laughs.

"I'm joking, but I mean it, Ian. I like bringing out the balls hanging on you. I bring out the balls on Dave."

Ian lifts a leg as though he's about to climb off my head, but then he lowers it and presses more of his weight on his balls. He rubs them over my cheeks and forehead and nose and eyes and mouth. He slaps me with his re-hardening dick. "I'm gonna ball your face again, Lenny." He's down my throat, whether I'm ready or not. I gag a little. He thrusts. I tell myself to relax. A few plunges, a few *Jesus goddamn Christ*s, and Ian gives me more cream.

When he climbs off my head, I sit up and grab him, kiss him. We stare into each other's eyes. I smile at the cockiness in his. "I like it when you assert yourself, Ian."

We get up from bed, and he dresses. Dave, at his desk, still wears only the snake T-shirt. He spoons corn flakes from a bowl and sorts student papers. Ian tells him bye.

"Later."

At our front door, I kiss Ian with my tongue in his mouth. I relish being naked in his arms. "Thanks for balling my face," I say. He laughs, pleased, and turns. In sunless gray haze, I watch his blue-jeaned butt sway down the walk to his car parked at the curb.

I pour a bowl of cereal, carry it into Dave's den, and wait for him to look up from a paper he's grading. I need to see his eyes so I can tell whether he heard Ian say he loves me. I'm cold. My nipples are so goose bumped they feel like pebbles under my skin. I want Dave to notice I'm still naked. I want Dave to be jealous. I want his eyes looking at me the way they did last night, like I'm a man he wouldn't want to lose. But he doesn't look up. God *damn* you, I think, and I head into the bathroom for a hot shower.

While I dress for work, Dave bends over his duffel bag, his muscular ass bare below his T-shirt. We both smell of soap and shaving cream. I watch him grab balls of socks, folded underwear, and dress shirts and pack them away. "I'll see you here at three, Dave?"

He nods.

"Give me a kiss, cowboy."

He gives me a fast kiss before turning to the dresser and opening a drawer.

I head to the back door and out into our chilly yard. The jade tree hedge is soaked with dew. I stop and watch a hummingbird hover in front of red blossoms on our bougainvillea. I wish I was going anywhere but the bookstore.

Jane types on her ergonomic keyboard as I come in and peel off my dark green sweater. Her new perfume reeks. The other day, Rosie amazed me by saying she likes it.

"You're here early, Jane."

"It's a good thing one of us is."

She wears her reading glasses and peers down at her

computer screen. I stuff my sweater into a desk drawer. "We don't open for ten minutes," I say. "With your trip to Aspen tomorrow, I'm surprised you came in at all today."

"I may not go to Aspen. I was up all night trying to pack. I don't have the right clothes for Colorado in April."

"Go shopping. You've got all day."

"I've been shopping all week. I don't need suggestions from someone who wears ties with washable trousers. And don't get near me if you have a cold."

"I don't have a cold."

"You sound hoarse."

"I dried out from the heater running last night." I'd love to tell her I'm hoarse from deep-throating Ian's cock.

She rises stiffly from her chair and struts out of our office to the stockroom. Her high heels match her salmon suit.

I mosey out to the cash register and find a note in Ian's small neat printing, about a book returned last night because of missing pages, which Ian suspects the customer razored out. Ian's more cynical than I am.

I hear the toilet flush, and Jane strolls out of the stockroom and along the customer side of the counter. She stops across from me, at the register.

"While I think of it, Leonard, I want the literary fiction moved back to the front of the store, where it belongs. You're not turning this place into a gift boutique."

"A gift boutique? You're the one who ordered the display of fuzzy key chains. I asked you before I moved the literary fiction."

"You caught me on my way out. I wasn't paying attention."

"Whose fault is that? People looking for the literary fiction find it. Best sellers are near the door, so everyone passes them. Best sellers *move*. That's why they're called *best sellers*."

"Don't try condescending to me, bub. You can't pull it off. If I go to Aspen, which I seriously doubt I will, I expect to see the store returned to normal when I come back."

"No way! Jane, have you passed Anaheim Books lately? Because they're having a going-out-of-business sale. Do you want to be next?"

"You're not literary-minded, Leonard, so you wouldn't understand, but to me one book like *A Tale of Two Cities* is worth all the others in this store. That's why I stay in the business. Both of my boys inherited my love of literature. If you ever wonder why my sons made something of themselves and you haven't, I suggest the answer may be as basic as reading habits."

"You're so full of shit, Jane! We moved the literary fiction before Christmas, and you haven't said a goddamn word about it until now."

"Don't start on me."

"You haven't read a fucking classic since college, and you probably read CliffsNotes then. You're in a tizzy getting ready for your goddamn trip, and you're taking it out on me. If you want a whipping boy, hire one. That's not my job. I'd give my right ball to be going on a nice spring vacation in the Rockies, and you turn it into a torture like all the rest of your fucked-up life."

Jane stomps into our office, her face so red she looks like she's about to pop.

I see Rosie just inside the store, key in hand. She looks sheepishly at me. "Do you want me to come back in a few minutes, Lenny?"

"Come in," I shout. "Join the party."

"Should I leave the door unlocked? It's nine o'clock."

"Sure, leave the fucking door unlocked. We never get a customer before ten, but we open *every* morning at nine. *Shit!*"

Rosie goes to the stockroom, eyes straight ahead of herself.

Jane stands crying behind her desk as I step into our office. I dig my fingers into my grimy, plasticized chair back. She bends over and yanks her purse from a drawer, storms around our desks, and rushes out of the office. Turning my head, I watch her hustle across the store floor. She pushes out the front door and hurries along the plate glass windows to the side parking area.

Her pink Cadillac rolls by the windows in the opposite direction. I'm still standing with my fingers digging into the chair. "You goddamn better go to Aspen," I mutter. I want to float in her pool with Ian's beautiful butt in my arms.

She didn't go on a tour of Portugal because she couldn't decide what to pack at the last minute. But her precious son wasn't waiting in Portugal.

She won't fire me, I tell myself, no matter what I said. She can't run the store.

❖

On the San Diego Freeway, in six lanes of stopped traffic near LAX, I'm still thinking of worse things I could have said to Jane. The air is a sunny white mélange of coastal haze and smog.

Dave's fidgety, bouncing his knees. He looks at his watch. I glance at the dashboard clock—it's quarter past four. His plane leaves at six.

"Don't worry, cowboy. You'll make it."

"I know."

Traffic starts moving. I keep my eyes on the brake lights of the car ahead.

"Are you planning to see Ian over the weekend?" Dave asks.

"I hadn't thought of it."

"I wish you were coming with me."

"So do I."

I hear the lie in my voice and hope he doesn't. I want Dave, and I want him to want me, but I want Ian, too.

❖

Driving back from the airport, I consider dropping by the bookstore to see Ian. At the last minute, I take the Brookhurst exit and go home for the night.

❖

I look out my office window, across the store to the parking lot, busy with Friday afternoon traffic. Ian, a handkerchief to his nose, pushes through the front doors and disappears into the stockroom. He walks behind the counter a few minutes later, his black bangs plastered in sweat above rheumy eyes and red nostrils.

"You don't look so well, Ian."

"I have a cold."

He doesn't sound like himself.

"I took some decongestant. I'm still stopped up, but now I'm half-asleep even though I slept all day. I feel like shit."

"Go home."

"Who'll close?"

"I'll stay. Dave's in Chicago. I'd just read a book at home anyhow. I'll read here. Don't come in tomorrow unless you feel a hell of a lot better."

He nods and starts back to the stockroom.

"Don't worry about your time card. I'll fix it."

"Thanks," he mumbles.

❖

Ian's at the store when I arrive to open in the morning. I figure he's here because, technically, part-timers aren't paid for sick leave.

"Get out of here, Ian. I'm paying you for last night, and I'll pay you for today. I've done the same for others."

"I slept fourteen hours," he says. "I can handle today. You don't want to work Saturday after working both the day and the evening on Friday. I'm only on till two, and Rosie will be here soon." He dabs a handkerchief at his chapped nostrils. "You shouldn't get close to me."

"I've already been close to you. You should go home and rest. Pick up some hot and sour soup on your way. I like hot and sour soup when I have a cold."

He climbs on the stool by the register. "I was planning to ask you over while I'm staying at Jane's house. With this cold, you probably wouldn't want to be around me."

"A little cold won't stop me when you feel like company. If you're sure you want to work, I'll go home for a while and bring you hot and sour soup at lunchtime. How's that?"

"How about bringing me hot and sour soup at Jane's house?"

"Sure." I bongo drum the counter a few times. "Will do."

❖

The sun shines on Jane's terra-cotta terrace, where Ian and I share soup and egg foo yung. He's blowing his nose more than eating. North Orange County spreads below us in haze, like a poster faded from sun until hardly any color or sharp line is left. Half of the swimming pool is visible over the terrace edge, the surface like a sheet of glass suspended above the sky blue bottom. A phone plays music, and Ian steps inside through open French doors. I keep eating while he talks to Melinda.

Ian returns carrying two towels. We poke down the railroad tie steps built into the cliff ablaze with yellow gazanias. The cement pool deck is chalk white in midday sun. Crows are cawing in the hillside chaparral, more summer brown than spring green. We undress without touching, sit on the warm, dark blue tile border wagging our feet in water tepid as a bath. Then we drop into the pool and hug the smooth, slick wall. I push back an arm's length in order to lean and kiss Ian's neck and shoulders. I avoid his mouth since he can't breathe through his nose.

We swim a few laps, and Ian stops. "I'm too tired to swim."

"Let's get out and lie in the sun."

We climb on the deck, and I dry him with a big yellow towel while he shivers. I pull faded green pads off two lounge chairs and lay the pads side by side on the cement. "Stay below the breeze," I tell him. Ian lies on his back, eyes closed, while I study his body in the warm sunshine. I press my tongue to the lines of skin of his flat navel. The dazzling afternoon light gives me an idea. I glance up at the sun and rotate Ian's cushion.

"Why are you moving me?"

"I want to see your anus in the sunlight."

He rolls on his stomach. I edge his feet apart, feeling their smooth soles with my thumbs. His small, tight buttocks are like marbles. I lie between his calves and widen his crack with my fingertips. His hole is a small, clean ring. I see it without shadow. I kiss his buttocks and gently finger his anus as he moans.

"Give me a second." I run up to the house and bring down a book bag with KY, condoms, and my toothbrush.

With both of us on our bellies, I lie between his legs and take a mental snapshot of his asshole in the sunlight. I'll be able to call up the picture whenever I want. With it in my mind's eye, I mount him and move my bone in and out slowly, feeling his ring squeeze me, feeling it ride over the rim between my shaft and my head. He squeezes me till the juice runs down my leg into the condom. I collapse on his buttocks and back and shoulders, and lie spread-eagled over him. I stay hard enough to not slip out, not all the way. When I'm ready to fuck him again, I withdraw and remove my condom. I flip him on his back and take his dick in my mouth. In a few moments, I swallow his cream.

The sun is low in the sky by the time Ian holds my hand and follows me up the flight of railroad tie steps to the patio. I lead him into the guest room in the house, stepping over a wadded red bathrobe on the floor when I put him to bed for a nap.

After carrying the remains of the soup and egg foo yung to Jane's refrigerator, I take a long hot shower in the lemon-scented guest bathroom, wallpapered in gold and cream, with a fluffy yellow rug on the floor and bars of soap wrapped in yellow tissue in a basket on the counter. I stand by a small window cranked open, toweling dry as I stare down at Jane's tiled garage roof and at the roofs of houses below hers along the ridge road.

Naked, I tour the living and bedrooms in fading daylight,

sinking my toes into thick beige carpet. I gaze at expensive couches, chairs, and bedspreads in pale shades of green and gold; at mahogany tables, desks, and dressers; and at seascapes and portraits on the walls. The rooms smell of heavy fabric and furniture polish.

In Jane's bedroom, high school graduation pictures of her sons stand in gilt frames on a dresser, both boys handsome in the well-cared-for way of affluent youth. I open a jewelry box on a vanity and take out a strand of pearls I recognize. Watching myself in the mirror, I fasten the choker around my neck.

Jane would shit if she saw me.

Ian hollers from the bedroom. I go and find him lying on his back with the covers kicked to the foot of the bed.

I ball his belly, our dicks between us. I savor the pearls on my otherwise naked body, wallow in their decorative feminine yin against my bare masculine yang. Ian and I both gush our seed between our chests. I lick my way down to his navel.

We fall asleep in each other's arms.

❖

Ian microwaves what's left of our Chinese food for dinner. Wrapped in blankets, we eat on the terrace and watch the shimmering distant lights. We start necking, which leads us back to bed for the night.

Ian isn't scheduled to work Sunday, so we spend the day between bed and kitchen. Our only contacts with the outside world are a message from Melinda asking if Ian still wants her to come to dinner tomorrow, and my daily chat with Dave. On Friday, I told him Ian has a cold so I worked in his place. "I suppose you and I may catch Ian's cold," I say on Sunday.

"Drink a lot of orange juice."

"I am."

In the background, I hear Dave's nephew laugh and yell in his deep sixteen-year-old voice, "For God's sake, Mom."

Dave's folks flew up from Cincinnati for the weekend. "We just took Mom and Dad to the airport," Dave says. "Wish you were here, Len."

"So do I," I mumble.

"I love you."

"Likewise." We sign off.

Ian kisses the back of my neck and wraps his arms around my stomach, settles a fingertip in my navel.

In bed, I tell Ian I love him. "I like having you all to myself."

"I like having you to myself, too."

❖

I call the bookstore from bed in the morning and tell Mai-Ly I'm not feeling well.

"Poor Lenny."

"Sweetie, I'm going to turn off my phone and get some more rest. I'll call later to see how things are going, all right?"

"All right, Lenny."

I look down at Ian's dark blue eyes smiling up, his lips wrapped around the head of my cock.

❖

We're naked in Jane's pool, bobbing like buoys. My throat has been getting sorer all day. Ian's still too stopped up to breathe through his nose, although he sounds more like himself when he talks.

"Melinda will be here soon," he says. "I should get out of the pool and make margaritas."

"I'll swim a few laps and be up to help."

"Take your time. We're having ready-made hamburger patties from Jane's freezer. I always eat whatever's in the house."

"You have such balls, Ian."

"She's never said anything."

I watch him climb out of the pool and stand dripping on the cement, drying himself with a gold designer label towel.

"What did you tell Melinda, anyhow?"

"Nothing. She knows you'll be here."

He wraps the towel around his waist; it reaches below his knees. I watch the soles of his feet as he climbs the railroad tie steps and disappears on the upper terrace.

I work up a sweat swimming laps and feel the endorphins in my system. This is my first exercise, other than sex, for three days.

As I climb out of the pool, I realize I didn't bring a towel down from the house. Shivering in the sun, shaking water droplets off my limbs, I look up and see Melinda peering down from the terrace. She turns her back and leans against the railing.

I climb the steps up the cliff, my nostrils stinging from chlorine, its antiseptic smell filling my head. As I step on the patio's sun-warmed tiles, Melinda glances at me, her eyes level with mine. She holds a margarita in a rocks glass, her long chestnut hair up, her statuesque frame clad in a white shell under pale denim overalls.

"I forgot to bring down a towel."

"Apparently."

I grin. I see Ian, in a black T-shirt and shorts, holding a phone to his ear in the kitchen. "Who's he talking to?"

"The painter working on his house. Don't let me keep you." She turns her back and looks down at the pool.

"You don't like me, do you?"

"I like you better with clothes on. I'd like you better still if you didn't wear a wedding ring."

"Fair enough."

I step into the kitchen.

Holding his phone to his ear, Ian watches a skillet, lifting and turning it to spread melting butter. "That'll be okay," he says. He smiles at my nakedness and motions to a pitcher of margaritas by a plate of salt on the sink counter. I turn a rocks glass upside down to coat the rim, fill the glass, and carry it into the bathroom. I shower, dry, and pull on shorts and a T-shirt.

We eat bleu cheeseburgers on English muffins at Jane's Shaker-style kitchen table. Melinda and Ian talk about Willa Cather, Melinda's specialty. I quote the beginning of *My Antonia*, and Melinda treats me like a dog performing a trick. She even says, "Good boy."

Ian laughs. I laugh and swallow the remainder of my third margarita.

We finish our burgers and sip tea with oatmeal cookies Melinda made. Conversation moves to Russian authors. I don't say much. I start to pour what's left in the margarita pitcher around the table, but I'm the only taker.

Ian pushes back in his chair. "Let's go sit in the living room."

"I should be on my way," Melinda says, looking at her watch. "I teach at nine in the morning, and I have preparation to do yet."

I begin clearing the table. The pungent smell of bleu cheese rising from our plates mixes with the sweet salty tang of margaritas in my mouth.

Melinda lingers, leaning against the kitchen counter, talking to Ian about the section of freshman lit Robert asked her to take over mid-semester when the instructor had surgery. Tomorrow, she's leading a discussion of *The Stranger*, a book I love.

Ian's quiet. I load the dishwasher. He blows his nose into a paper napkin.

"I suppose you have an early morning, too?" Melinda says, glancing in my direction.

"I don't have an early morning." I turn and press against Ian's backside, wrap my arms around his waist. Melinda looks away and picks up her purse from a chair.

While Ian walks her to the door, I pour several fingers of tequila in a rocks glass and squeeze a plastic lime over it.

Ian blows his nose again as he steps back into the kitchen. "How's your throat, Lenny?"

"Sore. Don't worry about it. I'm not."

"Thanks for cleaning up."

"Sure."

"Wait to start the dishwasher till I get out of the shower, please," he says. "Water pressure's shitty in this house."

I listen to the shower run and sip tequila at the kitchen table while pulling old credit card receipts out of my stuffed wallet. I come across the folded sheet with the Baltimore job ads on it and wad it up. A scrap of paper bearing Cleve's phone number floats to the floor.

Leaving the receipts and job ads page on the table, I carry the note and my drink into a pale gold den, where I sit at an ornate writing desk and dial Cleve's number on a faux antique phone. His recorded voice answers. I stare at a small oil seascape hanging above the desk and picture Cleve's king-sized bed floating over the dark green carpet of his room.

"Hi, Cleve, this is Lenny," I say at the tone. "Are you there? I just called to tell you I'm sorry about how things turned out between us. You're a nice guy."

Wondering if Cleve's sitting on his bed, staring at his phone and listening, gives me a boner.

"Call if you want, Cleve. We could still get together sometime."

I sign off and slip the scrap of paper into my pocket, while the shower cuts off across the house.

As I pass through the kitchen, I pull off my T-shirt and drop it, unzip my shorts and, with my engorged genitals sticking out through the fly, swagger along the hall to the guest bathroom, its small steamy space brimming with Ian's body. His skin is flushed from hot water and the big towel he's rubbing himself with. I poke his stomach with my dick. If I were a dog, I'd lie on my back and spread my haunches to show off my balls. I try to lift Ian, and we both start laughing and careen against the wall. I fall into his arms, and we kiss.

"I want to go to Baltimore with you. Take me instead of Dave."

"You're drunk," Ian says.

"I'm the one in love with you."

We stumble into the bedroom and into bed, where my head sinks deep into the pillow as the room slowly revolves.

"I love you," I say, closing my eyes. "I love you, I love you, I love you, I love you…"

❖

I wake and blink at a chink of sunlight along the edge of the curtain. My head is pounding, my throat raw. I roll over toward Ian. He's drowsing, his eyes not quite closed, his mouth near enough to envelop me in his morning breath.

I learned about men's morning breaths years ago: the cure comes in kissing. Moving my mouth close to Ian's, I breathe in the taste and kiss him. He squirms against me. I kick down the covers to free our feet, and our legs entwine. We press our torsos together. Ian rolls me on my back and sits up, straddling my full bladder.

"Did you mean what you said last night, Lenny?" He swoops down to kiss me again and sits back up, laughing. "You don't even remember what you said, do you?"

"I remember." I don't at first, but then I do. I said I wanted to go to Baltimore with him. I said I loved him, over and over. "I meant it." I'm so aroused at the moment, I'd follow him anywhere.

He scoots to the foot of the bed. I feel his testicles move along my leg like small animals. Kneeling on all fours, he catches my bobbing cock with his mouth. I stop myself short of coming and pull him up. "Ball my belly," I say. "I want to be under you, Ian." I crave his arms around me, his full weight bearing down on me, his flexing toes caressing my feet.

We shoot our loads between our chests and lie exhausted, sublimely gooey. The clock radio comes on, the traffic report telling us where freeways are backed up.

"We should make plans," Ian says.

"Right now, I need to get showered. I have to go to work today. And I have to piss like a racehorse."

Before I can move, Ian rolls off the mattress, pulls on the red bathrobe from the floor, and walks out of the room.

I get in the shower. I smell coffee while toweling dry. I get dressed and pad along the carpeted hall.

The kitchen's cool and dim, a breeze stirring the white curtain at the side of the window above the sink. Ian stands by the toaster, his back to me. Two glasses of orange juice and a bottle of Tylenol with its lid unsnapped sit on the table beside the credit card receipts and Dave's wadded job ads page I left there last evening.

"Do you want toast?" Ian says.

"Thanks."

I wash down three Tylenol with a swallow of orange juice, collect the job ads sheet and credit card receipts, and drop them into a trash can under the sink.

Wheat toast pops up, and Ian leans the slices against each other, tepee-fashion, on a saucer. He drops more bread into the slots. I pour a mug of coffee, sip it, and decide my stomach's too sour for coffee.

We eat toast standing in chilly, deep shade on the patio, the view gauzy. The murmur of traffic rises from the plain below like the buzz of insects, blending with the closer drone of the oil derrick, out of sight. The breeze carries a faint smell of something burning. Half the pool is dark blue in shade from the cliff, the other half crystal clear from sun slanting over the house roof and shining all the way to the bottom.

I glance at Ian and put my arm around his waist. "We'll make plans, Ian."

"You're just saying that. It's okay. I know this was a lark for you. Dave gets home tonight, and your life goes on as usual."

"I don't know what happens from here. We'll plan what happens, you and me."

❖

I consider going home on my lunch hour to nap, but I drink a large coffee and buy throat lozenges at a drugstore.

Tony's working out at the gym. We avoid each other.

As I head into the locker room to shower, he's behind

me—not by accident, I suspect. We undress without making eye contact. I'm nervous. I shouldn't have called him an asshole. I'm not a fist fighter, I'm a hotheaded fool, even now full of enough macho pride to follow tauntingly close on his heels into the electric yellow shower room. I stop by a stall with a nozzle that usually works better than some others.

"Are you still pissed at me?" he asks.

"Are you still avoiding me?"

He unwraps his towel, hangs it on a hook, and glances down at himself. My eyes involuntarily follow for a glimpse at his uncut meat. He holds out his hand. "Are we okay?" he says. He grins. "Just don't shake the wrong thing."

I laugh aloud, and we shake hands.

I watch Tony's broad foot under the metal partition between our stalls as I shower. I watch his heel lift and fall on the wet tile, his toes gripping and flexing as soapy water splashes over them.

We dry at the same time, without talking. "There's something I want to explain," he says while we're dressing. "Outside."

"Sure."

We finish assembling ourselves, and I follow him from the locker room and gym. In the middle of the parking lot, he faces me and steps backward, up on a curbed planter with a palm tree rising as tall and straight as a telephone pole. As I look up at him, a jet crosses high in the white sky.

"I'm not gay," Tony says. "I'm not even bi. But if you and I were marooned on an island, alone…do you know what I'm saying? That threw me at first. Then I started thinking about an ugly, out-of-shape woman versus a good-looking well-built guy."

"So what?" I say. "I could do it with a woman, marooned

on an island. It doesn't mean I want women. And we're not marooned. There are plenty of gay men for me to fuck. I slept with one behind my lover's back last night."

As the words come out of my mouth, I realize how desperate I am to confess. I don't want to be doing things behind Dave's back. I love Dave. Maybe I love Ian, too. Maybe I could love Cleve, if it comes to that.

"How'd you get by with it?"

"Dave's out of town."

Tony takes a deep breath. The smooth planes of his snug dress shirt rise and fall. He looks past me to the gym. "There's a little brunette in my office. Her husband left her with a one-year-old. I want her *so bad*, Lenny—so really fucking *bad*. And I know she wants me. But I don't know how I'd face Tess afterward."

"If you don't know how you'd face your wife, you'd better not do it."

"I'm in hell."

"I'm always in hell." My mind flashes to Ian lying by Jane's pool. "Except when I'm in heaven." I grin and shake my head. "Speaking of hell, the bookstore needs me."

Tony steps off the planter curb, and we turn in different directions to our cars.

❖

Dave's flight from Chicago arrives at quarter of nine. I'm in the baggage area. We tell each other where we are on our phones. A kid near me eats popcorn, the buttery smell making me want some. "I see you," Dave says. I see him, too, head and shoulders above the crowd between us, his brown hair ruffled on the side, from sleeping against the plane window, I figure. He wears a navy pullover, gray slacks, and sneakers. He rolls a black suitcase beside him, his flat, traveling briefcase dangling from his other arm. He squeezes past a bottleneck in the crowd to reach me, hugs me and pats my ass.

"So your paper went all right?" I say as we walk outside.

"I'll get a publication out of it."

"Diane, Trev, and your folks are okay?"

"Fine."

Dave asks how things were here.

"I read a lot."

We said all these things on the phone while he was there. We cross the road from the terminal to the parking garage, find the car, and throw Dave's stuff in the rear. As we inch up to the freeway in stop-and-go traffic, I keep my gaze fixed on the taillights of a truck ahead. "Ian came to work today. He's feeling better. I think I have his cold."

"You sound stopped up."

"I felt worse this morning. I should have taken a lunch hour nap instead of going to the gym. You may want to avoid intimate contact with me for a day or two."

"I'll take my chances." Dave rests a hand along the inseam of my jeans, and I feel my libido coming alive. "I've got something I want to give you," he says.

I'm in bed under Dave before we've been home ten minutes, his big biceps and wiry forearms hugging my head like he's afraid of dropping it. He feeds me a nipple while he bones the hollow of my chest. His balls feel like ripe peaches. His big toes caress my calves. "I love you, Len." He brings his cock up to my mouth and spurts more cream than I knew a man could. I swallow, licking the inside of my mouth, tasting and collecting the last of his seed while he finishes me off with his strong hand.

I wake later in our dark bedroom, my nostrils and throat dry, the pleasant doughy taste of Dave's semen in my mouth.

The heater fan cycles off, and the house is silent. A few cars pass on Brookhurst, their tires hissing on wet pavement. I hear rain faintly pattering the roof—an April shower.

I glance at the clock radio. *The Tonight Show* just went off. Ian watches it.

Easing out of bed, I tiptoe to the kitchen and carry my phone close to the back door, as far from our bedroom as I can get and be inside. I select Ian's name on my contact list. He doesn't pick up. I hear his message center start to play as our kitchen light flashes on. "Who are you calling?" Dave says.

"No one. The store's answering machine, to see if it works. Jane said it didn't. I meant to check before." I point at the roof as I turn off my phone. "It's raining."

Dave takes milk out of the refrigerator. "Do you want some?"

I nod, and he pours two glasses, returns the carton to the refrigerator. We drink our milk.

"Aren't you coming back to bed?" he says.

I follow him, switching off the light. He puts his arm around me and pulls me to his side.

6. OIL AND WATER

Smelling mucus from my stopped-up nose, I trail Dave across paving stones through the dichondra and topiary front yard of Robert's white stucco house. The stones are mushy with jacaranda petals from a neighbor's tree farther up the hill. I carry a bottle of merlot, and Dave a six-pack of beer.

While we wipe our shoes on a bristly welcome mat, the wine-red door opens. Robert's obese art historian friend, Lila, smiles at us, her black hair pulled back, her eyebrows and lashes heavily mascaraed. "Keep wiping, boys. Robert's having his annual jacaranda snit." Lila's voice is husky, and her burst of laughter melodic. She knows how to dress for her size, an untucked loose magenta blouse flowing over a matching ankle-length skirt.

"Stunning outfit, Lila." Looking her up and down, I whistle softly.

"You like?" She bats her eyelashes in mock coquetry while Dave picks a jacaranda petal off my white knit shirt. "Come in, boys."

Stepping into the sandstone foyer, we hear a hubbub of voices from the rear of the house. Lila hugs Dave, but I move out of her reach when she turns to me. "I have a cold."

"I just got over a pip of a cold. Come here, blondie." She

gives me a squeeze. "Now excuse *moi* while I hit the head. Everyone's in the kitchen or family room."

Lila floats down a hall off the far end of the long living room. Dave follows me to the dining table, spread with casserole dishes and large wood salad bowls under plastic wrap. An open pantry door blocks our way into the kitchen. When the door closes I'm nose-to-nose with Melinda, whose eyes flit past my shoulder to Dave before she smiles at me. "Why, hello. I almost didn't recognize you out of a pool with your clothes on."

"Glad to see you, too," I mumble.

"Sounds like you caught someone's cold."

Melinda turns sideways to let me pass.

I set our bottle of wine with others on the butcher block island in the middle of the kitchen and smile at Robert, talking to a woman almost as short as he is—his niece, I assume; her visit from Alaska is the reason for this party. She wears a simple black sleeveless dress and a necklace of black beads. Shoulder-length loose brown hair frames her pretty face with faintly etched lines and little makeup.

Robert flashes his smiling gray eyes at me, and he touches my forearm with his small hand. "Hello, Lenny, hello, Dave. I want you to meet Ruth."

"You live in Anchorage," Dave says. "Cool."

The lids of Ruth's brown eyes crinkle as she laughs. "Almost *cold* sometimes! You're the Twins player. My ex-husband and I went to a lot of Twins games when we lived in Minneapolis."

"I was on a farm team and quit for graduate school after two unspectacular seasons."

A towheaded girl standing behind Ruth's legs chews the ear of a stuffed pink dog. I stoop down to her eye level. "And who are you, may I inquire?"

She moves behind the skirt of Ruth's dress.

"This is Kelly," Ruth says. Kelly peeks at me from around a small fistful of her mother's skirt.

"Pleased to meet you, Kelly. What's your dog's name?"

She lets the dog's ear fall free from her teeth and stares at me.

I wink. As I rise to my feet, I'm bumped by a brunette girl just old enough to be forming breasts. "*Mom*, I can't find my blue dress! You *did* pack it, didn't you?"

"Yes, I *packed* it. Calm down, Sarah." Ruth rolls her eyes while Sarah tugs her from the kitchen, little Kelly trailing, hanging on her mother's hem and staring over her shoulder at me.

"What was that crack Melinda made about a swimming pool?" Dave says in my ear.

"She said I caught someone's cold. Maybe Ian told her he fools around with us."

"In a swimming pool?"

"I don't know where she got that. Why are we standing in the kitchen when it's so crowded?"

"I want to get a beer."

"I'll be in the other room." I squeeze out of the kitchen and glance around the living room for Ian, spotting him with a group on the far side. For the past four days we haven't been together, except innocently at the store. Robert's house is chilly. Ian wears a tight black T-shirt tucked into jeans, showing off his nipples. His feet are bare. I watch his clean, smooth toes flexing on the rug and almost come. He sees me and grins. I take a seat by Lila on the couch and ask where she and Robert are going for their summer travels. They've been all over the world together.

"Madrid first, to spend a week in the Prado."

While Lila tells me about the Prado, prompted by my

good-listening act, I let Ian's dark blue eyes bore into me. He and I almost whine, we want so much to sniff each other.

"After Madrid, we're spending six weeks in a friend's London flat."

I keep Lila talking about some woman in London with a gated neighborhood park. I want Ian to fuck me so bad my asshole's turning inside out.

Lila stops talking and glances over her shoulder at Ian.

"Where will you and Robert be staying in London?" I say.

Lila laughs with a snort. "Why, at the flat of the woman I just finished telling you all about!"

"I didn't realize you'd be staying with her."

"Staying with her? When she's teaching a summer class at our beloved institution and house-sitting for Robert?"

"Sorry—this decongestant I'm taking affects my concentration."

"*Something's* affecting your concentration." Laughing, Lila scoots to the edge of the couch, pushing herself off with ring-laden fingers. Her magenta blouse and skirt billow like a cloud as she glides away from me.

"Time to eat," Robert shouts to the room. "Everything's hot."

I rise and shuffle into a serving line that goes around the dining table. Talking across it, I ask Ian where his shoes are.

"My new sneakers rubbed a blister on my heel," he says.

Holding a plate of enchiladas and rice doused with enough hot sauce to clear my sinuses, I sit, legs folded, on the living room floor by Dave. Ian goes into the family room. Melinda settles on a hassock near Dave and me, a plate balanced on the knees of her green slacks. "The two of you in the same place at the same time—that's something I thought I'd never see." Melinda smiles.

I watch Ian standing by a fireplace filled with potted green plants. He and some other grad student laugh and set their plates on the mantel, holding their flexed arms side by side to compare muscles. Jesus Christ, Ian, I think, as I look at his balled biceps, could you possibly torture me more?

Robert and his niece, sitting together on the bench of a piano in a corner of the room, laugh in our direction. Kelly, the smaller of Robert's great-nieces, the little blonde, in pajamas is toddling to me. She stops at the toe of one of my black-and-brown oxfords. "She wants *you* to tuck her in," Ruth says.

"Me, huh?" I smile.

"Kelly, honey, he's eating."

Kelly takes hold of my little finger and yanks, while Melinda and Dave laugh. I rise to my feet and set my plate on an end table. Ruth walks over to us. I catch the scowl of Kelly's pubescent sister, who tosses her head and sets her ponytail swinging. "I'm not experienced at this," I tell Ruth.

"That's not what I hear," Melinda murmurs.

Dave avoids looking at Melinda or me, I notice.

"Can Mommy come with you?" Ruth asks her daughter.

Kelly tugs me over to the hallway amid adult chuckles.

While Ruth tucks her daughter into lavish covers on a sleigh bed way too big for a little girl, I hover by an antique dresser on which sits a pastel lantern illuminating geese in flight. Ruth kisses her daughter's forehead, and I wink at my admirer.

I look back as I leave the room and see Kelly staring at me in the dim light.

After I finish eating, I join Sandy and her friend, Janine, standing by the stone table in Robert's small, bamboo-enclosed backyard. While the women smoke, they tell me about a neighbor in Sandy's condo complex. "He throws me a bone now and then, pun intended," Sandy says. "I know nothing about him—background, family, occupation. He says he has 'business interests.' He sells heroin at elementary schools for all I know."

"Tell Lenny the sweet thing he said to you last week," Janine says.

Sandy waves away Janine's suggestion as though shooing a fly.

I once thought Janine—a tall, beaky computer programmer—was a closet lesbian with a crush on Sandy. Then Janine got drunk at a beach picnic and told me about her ex-boyfriend's cock with enough loving detail to make me wonder if she wasn't really a gay man.

"Jeff maintains I'm too quick to find fault in romance," Sandy says. Jeff is Sandy's son, a junior at Cal Poly San Luis Obispo. I know Jeff to be a sweet guy, manly enough to make it into my fantasies if I don't keep my guard up. I'm glad he's straight and will never be a temptation.

I excuse myself to take a leak, watching for Ian on my way to the bathroom. Dave and Brian, the engineering professor, sit in the den off the living room, just as they did at Robert's last party. The only other people in the room are two women admiring a seascape.

I come out of the john, and Ian waits to get in. We watch each other in the hallway like animals unsure whether to flee or fight. I lean toward him, and we kiss. I push him against the wall, and we dig our fingertips into each other's hair, caressing each other's scalps as though molding them in clay.

A shadow moves, and we jump apart. Inches from us, Dave's buddy, Brian, stares at the carpet.

Ian steps into the bathroom and closes the door. I slide by Brian. He eyes me admonishingly.

"Fuck," I mutter under my breath.

"Fuck *me*?" His straight-shooting voice resonates with incredulity.

"No, I said 'fuck,' not 'fuck you.'"

"I've always thought you were a nice guy, Lenny. Don't turn into a shit."

Someone comes up behind me. I keep my eyes on Brian. "Did anyone ever say you look like a young Paul Newman?" I slur my words, like I had too much to drink and that's why I kissed someone at a party. Brian looks annoyed by my pretense. As I move along, I realize I'm screwing up tonight.

Not sure of where to haunt, I pick up one of three remaining earthenware dinner plates—all the dessert plates have been used—and scoop up the last piece of a two-layer carrot cake. I eat my cake alone by the table, glancing at people talking in groups in the living room. I wonder if Dave is by himself in the den.

Ian walks past me, from the john. I want to kiss him so badly I can taste his saliva. He wanders into the family room.

I step into the kitchen with my empty cake plate. The dishwasher whirs and whooshes. Robert's niece leans against the sink counter, her profile to me. She wags a finger at Robert's nose while he giggles, his bald pate shining under a ceiling spot lamp. Catching sight of me, he looks startled. I wonder why.

"Confess, Uncle Robert," his niece says. "I thought it was the ballplayer, but you're in love with the blond."

Me, I realize. Robert's small face withers. Ruth glances my way and freezes, mouth open, finger still pointing at Robert. I lower my eyes to the bottles of wine and cans of soft drinks on the butcher block island between us.

"Your little blonde's a cutie, all right," I say, feigning to have misheard. "Not that your older girl isn't cute, too. I believe there's beer in the fridge?" I saunter around the island, add my plate to others in the sink, and take a beer from the refrigerator. "Great party, Robert."

"Glad you're enjoying it." His face is beet red.

"Dave and I want to have a party at our place soon. We hardly see Sandy since she moved to Laguna Niguel. She says Jeff will be home for summer. Maybe we'll have a cookout when he gets here, before you and Lila take off."

Robert nods. His niece turns to the sink and runs water over stacked plates. I glance at her back, in the modest sleeveless black dress.

"I think I'll go find Dave, see what he's doing."

"He and Brian were talking baseball in the den," Robert says.

"The macho guys."

Robert and I smile. His face is less red.

I carry my beer out to the dwindling groups in the living room. People have begun leaving. I swill my beer and find Dave standing alone in a corner of the den staring at baseball on a silent TV. The game's in extra innings. On Dave's handsome face is a shadow of anguish I've glimpsed before when I come upon him watching baseball by himself. I take his hand. I wish Brian hadn't seen me kissing Ian.

"I'm ready to go whenever you are, cowboy. I can wait if you want to see the end of the game."

"No." Dave switches off the TV.

We find Robert in the family room and hug both him and Sandy. Robert's niece isn't with them. Robert smiles at Dave and avoids my eyes.

While he and Dave talk, I escape from the house into the cool night. I'm behind the wheel of our coupe, parked along the curbless road, when Dave catches up. "I turned around and you were gone," he says.

"I thought you were right behind me."

Rather than head up the grade beyond Robert's house and snake home through the hills, I make a U-turn and descend to the old mission-style high school. Dave looks over at me as we crawl through the historic center of Fullerton, where lights twinkle in the trees and tipsy revelers walk between restaurants and bars. "Did you see much of Ian tonight, Len?"

"Not really."

"What's with Melinda?"

"Melinda is weird."

I sing along in falsetto to a song on the radio. I remember singing hymns in falsetto at the Methodist church I went to with Michael, making his grandmother and her friends giggle. His mother thought I was a wise-ass, which I was at seventeen. Despite my wise-assness, his mother couldn't resist me until she caught Michael and me in bed together.

Crossing town, I have a boner for Ian that Dave will benefit from as soon as we get home. I plan it. We'll get naked in the living room, and I'll go down on my knees. Already I look forward to swallowing Dave's cum. If I'm a shit to him at times, I'm good to him, too, I tell myself.

❖

I remain sitting on the washing machine after my Sunday morning talk with my mom, my phone still in my hand as it rings.

"When can I see you, Lenny?" Ian asks.

"Come over tonight. Come for dinner."

"I don't know."

Dave steps into the kitchen carrying his Georgetown mug. He glances at my swinging feet, my bare heels rhythmically thumping the enamel.

"Maybe not dinner," Ian says. "I'd have to talk too much."

"Around ten?"

"It'll feel weird."

"It won't. Ten should be fine." I glance at Dave. "Ian's coming over tonight." Dave doesn't react. "Good," I say into the phone.

"If you really think so," Ian says.

"See you tonight."

"I don't know."

"Bye, Ian."

As I hang up, I spot a few ants crawling on the floor near the back door. I hop off the washer, tear a paper towel from the roll, and wipe them up. Dave watches me as I turn around.

"Len, are you certain you want Ian coming over tonight?"

"Sure, why not?"

"Last time he came over, you shoved me against the refrigerator and told me to fuck off."

"I'd had a bad day. I got over it."

"Maybe we should stop seeing Ian."

"I don't *want* to stop seeing Ian!"

"Just a suggestion—you don't have to raise your voice."

"You started this, Dave. You can't end it just because you don't like Ian and I having feelings for each other."

"Whatever you say. But no more shoving."

He refills his coffee mug and carries it out of the kitchen.

"Go to hell, Dave."

He glances back and gives me a superior look, like a parent rising above an annoying child. I try to return it but know I only appear foolish.

❖

Ian talks to Dave more than I talk to either of them as we suck on bottles of beer in the living room. When Dave goes into the bathroom, Ian and I kiss.

My phone rings as Dave steps back into the living room—Rosie from the store.

"Lenny, I'm sorry to bother you, but I can't find my keys to close up. I know they're here somewhere. I've looked and looked."

"Relax, sweetie. I'll be right there."

I hang up and grab my wallet from the bedroom. Dave is opening fresh beers as I hustle out the back door.

Rosie and I look all over the bookstore but can't find her fuzzy orange key ring. Because her car keys are on the lost ring, I drive her to her apartment in Yorba Linda, a forty-minute round trip for me.

When I step in the kitchen door at home, my bladder about to burst, I don't hear Dave and Ian talking.

They aren't in the living room. Glancing into our bedroom on my rush to the john, I freeze for an instant and watch Dave's bare backside and Ian's raised heels on our double bed. As I pull one sneaker off, I hop into the bathroom and then unzip my jeans just in time. My urine flows on and on. I hear Dave coaxing Ian, calling him *lover*. I peel off my T-shirt and use the toes of my one bare foot to anchor the sneaker I'm wearing so I can get out of it. I shake off my last drops of pee.

Shrugging one leg out of my jeans, I stumble to the bedroom doorway while Ian mutters *Jesus Christ* over and over. He groans in orgasm as I balance against the doorjamb, trying to disentangle my second foot from my pant leg and underwear. Dave's buttocks clench as his big, lean body spasms. I watch him collapse on Ian and bury his face in Ian's neck. Dave rolls himself and Ian over, so Ian lies on Dave's chest. Ian's eyes are closed. Dave lolls his head so his eyes meet mine. While we stare at each other, he nuzzles Ian's hair and gives him small repeated kisses on the crown.

You son of a bitch, I think, glaring at Dave. I shake my foot out of my wadded jeans and underwear and kick them along the hall floor.

I take a beer out of the refrigerator, open it and bang the bottle on the countertop so hard beer spews out like a geyser. I hear the bedroom door close, listen to the hall floor creak, and then Dave pissing, Dave washing up.

He pads into the kitchen. I jerk my knee at his balls, and he shoves me, pins my shoulders to the refrigerator door. "You tried to knee me!" he hisses. "You goddamn better say you're sorry!"

"Fuck you, motherfucker!"

"I'm sick of your one-sided shit, Len! You have to be the one getting it, don't you? How did you ever become such a spoiled fucking brat?"

I spit in his face, and he knees me.

He lets go of my shoulders. I bend over and hug my balls. They feel like they're in my belly. My butt slides down along the refrigerator door, to the floor.

He turns and stamps out of the kitchen. I wait for the ache to stop.

Dave's out of sight, and the bedroom door is shut when I skulk into the hall, my face wet with tears of anger more than pain. He didn't knee me nearly as hard as he could have, but I'm less than grateful. With a blanket from the linen closet, I fall on the guest room couch and bury my face in the sofa back.

It's daylight when I open my eyes. I'm amazed. I can't believe I slept all night. I sit up on the couch, stand, then stumble into the hallway. The shower runs behind the closed bathroom door. Our bedroom door is ajar, Ian under the bedcovers on his stomach.

The sound of the shower stops. The bathroom door opens,

and steam flows out. I step into the room. Dave takes a razor from the medicine cabinet and wipes the mirror with his towel. I watch his foggy reflection as he spreads gel on his cheeks and chin. While I piss, I mumble, "I'll shower while you're shaving."

He ignores me.

I reach behind the white plastic curtain and turn on the water. As I hold a hand under the cold spray, I hear Ian yawn. Tousle-haired and sleepy-eyed, he stretches in the bathroom doorway. "What happened to you last night, Lenny? I thought you were coming to bed. I fell aslee—"

"I took Rosie home and went back to search the parking lot for her keys."

"Where'd you sleep?"

"I dozed off reading in the guest room."

Frowning from me to Dave, Ian steps between us and stands over the toilet. While he pisses, I step into the tub and pull the shower curtain. Hot water streams down my back. I hear Dave tell Ian to help himself to coffee and cereal.

"I'm going home to sleep more," Ian says. The toilet flushes, and for a moment my water is hotter. "See you later, Lenny," Ian calls.

Eyes closed, I tip my head back and let the water flow through my hair.

"Lenny?"

"I heard you."

❖

I'm reading *Modern Architecture* near the windows in the bookstore when I notice cars in the parking lot casting long shadows.

Back at my desk, I glance at the cover of a report the

accountant left while I was at the gym. Mai-Ly said he wants
to talk to Jane and me—I assume about the store losing money.
We've always had a post-Christmas slump, but this one has
lasted until April.

Seeing Ian's shadow in my doorway, I lean forward in my
chair and keep my eyes on the accountant's report. When Ian's
shadow lingers, I turn a page.

"Lenny, you're the one who said I should come over last
night. I told you I didn't want to talk to Dave. What did you
expect me to do with him?"

"Put him off till I got home?"

"If you could come to my house, we wouldn't have this
problem."

"How about tonight? I'll come to your house."

"What'll you tell Dave?"

"Fuck Dave."

"I don't want him to hate me."

"What do you care if you're in love with me? I'll worry
about Dave."

Ian cracks his knuckles and leans against the doorframe.

"I'll see you around ten thirty," I say. "At your house."

Closing the accountant's report, I open my phone calendar
and stare at it until Ian walks away.

He's with a customer as I leave. I wave in his direction
without slowing down.

At home, Dave eats pork chops and applesauce at our
dining table. We glance at each other as I walk by him. He
wears basketball trunks and a tank shirt.

Taking off my work clothes, I notice our bank statement
among the mail on the dresser. One of us should go online and
move some money into savings. I usually do it.

"I fried pork chops," Dave hollers. "I waited for you until
I was starving."

"I stopped at McDonald's." I clear my throat. "Thanks."

In my jeans and Haverford sweatshirt, I wander back to the living room. Dave's wiping a chunk of wheat bread around his plate, circling pork chop bones. He chews and swallows.

"Are your balls okay, Len? I barely kneed you."

"Thanks for the kindness."

"You spit in my face." He gets up from the table, picks up his empty plate. "I can't believe you spit in my face. We need to talk, Len. I've been thinking about it all day. Ian's like a drug we're addicted to, and the addiction's fucking up our lives."

I step into the kitchen, fork two pork chops from a skillet on a waiting plate, and cover it with tin foil. Dave carries his empty plate into the room. I put the covered pork chops in the refrigerator. "I'm going out for a while. Remember that guy Cleve? He asked if I wanted to have a drink. I ran into him at the gym."

"At the gym? I thought he lives in Newport Beach."

"He goes to my gym when he calls on customers up here. I've never seen him there before."

"I'll bet. Are you planning to sleep with him or have you already?"

"I might sleep with him."

"Do whatever the fuck you want. We both know you will."

"Like you don't?"

"Just make sure whatever you do is safe, Len. Don't do something stupid because you're pissed off at me." Dave pads into his den and closes the door.

As I cross the backyard on my way out, I glance at the drawn drape of his lighted window. My hatchback's parked in the alley, snug along our pink block wall. A security lamp on a garage across the alley flashes on. I unlock my car door as a neighbor's cat darts by my feet, and I jump. The cat sails up on our wall and faces me, its green eyes glowing.

I don't relax until I'm inside Ian's house, glancing around the all-beige front room, empty except for a TV on a metal stand wheeled into a corner. The only other time I was here, the night I helped carry his mother to bed, the place was a wreck, crammed with old furniture with dirty dishes and magazines piled on it. Now the house reeks of new carpet and paint. Burlap-looking drapes on shiny gold hoops and a shiny gold rod cover the picture window. "It looks completely different," I say.

Ian nods. "The Realtor said to paint and carpet in neutral colors."

"What did you do with all the furniture?"

"Threw it out. I kept the kitchen barstools and my bedroom stuff."

I pry off my deck shoes and feel the rug with my toes. Ian wears a plaid flannel shirt and cords and is barefoot. He leads me into the hall and motions to two empty rooms. A third room has a single bed with a tan spread, a cardboard dresser, and a small blond desk, grimy and glass-ringed.

Ian fills two jelly glasses with white wine, which we carry to a pair of webbed folding chairs on the patio. Dave and I have identical chairs from the drugstore. A leggy, tree-height poinsettia rises from a patchy lawn surrounded by a dilapidated wood fence. Ian pulls a joint from his shirt pocket and lights it. He takes a hit and passes it to me. "I'll have money after I sell this place. You can take your time, find a job you like in Baltimore."

I look up through the sparse branches of the poinsettia, to a half moon.

"Where'd you tell Dave you were going tonight?"

"I said some guy at the gym asked me out for a drink."

He considers this, takes his turn with the joint, and passes it to me again.

"You could move away with that guy. Dave doesn't have to know you're going with me."

"He'll know sometime."

"Maybe he'll be with someone else by then." Ian frowns.

"Let's not talk about Dave," I rasp, exhaling.

In our marijuana buzz, we start kissing. Our toes find each other's. With tongues in one another's mouths we rise and stumble, lips locked together, into the house and to Ian's single bed. We crowd on the mattress that smells of his adolescence and young manhood. I'm sure he doesn't notice the scent. I want to make love to him on this bed for the rest of my life. I want to move in and live with him in the room he grew up in. We lie kissing until he turns around, head at my crotch. He takes one of my balls in his mouth, and I take one of his. We each move back and forth, ball to ball. My dick throbs insanely as Ian makes me feel my balls, while I do the same for him. He breathes, "Take my cock, Lenny!" His first gush hits my face before I get his cock in my mouth. He wraps his lips around my head, and I instantly cream for him.

We lie with each other's sated, fleshy wieners in our mouths. I imagine being in this bed with him at sixteen, as Michael and I were in my boyhood bed in Texas. But when Ian was sixteen, I was twenty-one, and he didn't have sex with a guy until he was twenty-four and noticed Dave in the college weight room and realized Dave noticed him. He appeared in Dave's office in a tank shirt that wouldn't cover both his nipples. He wanted to know about Dave's ecology class, which supposedly he was thinking of auditing. Dave told me the story.

Ian and I get hard again in each other's mouths. He lets my cock slip out. "I want to watch you come, Lenny." He switches on the desk lamp and folds the bed's single pillow, propping it against the wall behind his head. I kneel with a knee on each side of his ribs. I reach behind my butt to stroke his cock while he strokes mine. I shoot between his eyes, then on his forehead, then on his cheek. He smears my cream around. "I may never wash my face again," he says. I sheathe his cock and sit on it, and rock and roll and rise and fall. My anus bites him. *Jesus fuck*, he moans.

After he comes, I smile and tell him I love making him swear.

I'm still high and elated driving home on broad Orangethorpe Avenue with only a few cars in sight. The strip malls hover dark under their tall parking lot lamps. The Methodist church that reminds me of Michael looms ghostlike from its landscaped grounds, a light shining up at its modern cross.

Dave's either asleep or pretending to be. I climb in my side of our bed, and he rolls to me and kisses me. He finds my hand and holds it. I wait till I can tell by his breathing that he's asleep, and then I let his fingers slip away.

❖

"I ran into Ian in the dining commons," Dave says as we're eating grilled hamburgers in evening sun on the patio. "He said he and Melinda have tickets for something at the Music Center this coming weekend."

I nod and keep chewing.

While we're cleaning up the kitchen, I mention I have a date with Cleve. "I told him I'd sleep over."

Dave takes a Pepsi from the refrigerator and snaps it open. I'm standing close enough to feel the sticky vapor rise from the can's mouth. He walks over to the kitchen doorway, stops, and turns around.

"If you want to know the truth, I thought that guy was an asshole the night you brought him here," Dave says. Then he closes his eyes and frowns. "Fuck it. I didn't think he was an asshole."

❖

I sleep with Ian, go to work from his house, then sleep a night at home.

After supper Friday, I leave for Ian's at dusk. He won't be home yet. The other two nights I was supposedly seeing Cleve, I left our house near ten. But Dave knows Ian gets off work at ten, so I'm leaving home earlier tonight.

I don't know where to go in the meantime.

On La Palma Avenue, I follow a midsized Chevy, two teenage couples dressed for a prom inside. We're about to pass a shopping center, and I turn in.

At a clothing store, I buy a forest green shirt, marked down and hanging on a sale rack. It costs next to nothing. The color will look great with Ian's black hair and dark blue eyes.

I pull up beside his car in his driveway. As I open my door, he leans out of the house and hollers, "It *sold*! The Realtor called me at the bookstore just after you left!"

"Wow. So fast?"

He holds his arms open for me to hug him. I try to act as excited as he is.

A bottle of cheap champagne and two empty juice glasses sit in the middle of the living room's pristine carpet. Ian walks over and lowers the volume of the ten o'clock news, blaring from the TV in the corner.

"I'm rich! At least compared to what I was." He eyes the clothing bag in my hand.

"I bought you something. I got a boner picturing you in it."

He lets the sack float to the floor while he holds up the shirt. After pulling out several pins, he undoes the buttons, peels off his T-shirt, and slips on my present.

"Don't button it," I say, taking his hands and kissing the hollow of his chest. I wrap my arms around his back, inside the shirttail, and pull him to me. Kissing, we shuffle into his room.

I'm heartsick he sold the house. As I make love to him, I breathe deep through my nostrils behind his ears, under his arms, between his scrotum and his groin. He'll never smell as strong as he smells here, in his room, on his own old mattress.

After sex, we eat spaghetti with butter and Parmesan cheese at the kitchen bar. We sip the champagne. The house is chilly. I wear the red bathrobe that lay wadded in a ball on the floor during most of our time at Jane's house. Ian wears his black and orange rugby shirt and shorts. A ship is sinking on TV across the living room. Ian curls his foot atop mine, bent over a stool rung.

"So will you be ready to move by June?" he says.

"I thought school starts in August?"

"I have to clear out of the house on June sixteenth."

I sprinkle more Parmesan cheese on my pasta and fumble strands around my fork.

He watches me. "Neither of us wants to hurt Dave," he mumbles with his mouth full. "Maybe we're kidding ourselves."

"June is earlier than I expected, that's all."

On TV, people on the ship scream.

❖

Our empty coffee mugs sit on the kitchen counter beside last night's crusty spaghetti plates. Saturday morning cartoons play on Ian's TV as I step out his front door into hazy sunshine. Ian is in the shower. Royal Books will open late. Rosie will get to the store before him.

I pull up at home, and Dave, in a tank shirt and shorts, kneels on our front lawn by a sprinkler head, a screwdriver in his hand. I had hoped he'd be jogging. He stands up and watches me walk up to him. "We need to replace this whole sprinkler system," he says. "We could do it ourselves, put sprinklers in the backyard, too."

"We could do a lot of things." I shrug and move along into the house. He follows and hovers behind me.

"I can't live like this, Len."

"Like what?"

"With you out half the time."

"Why don't we go for a run and talk about it later? I haven't been home two minutes."

He pads into the bedroom, looking peeved.

I pour a glass of orange juice and drink it as I gaze out the kitchen door window. Our wet season is over, and rain won't fall again for months. Since our back lawn has no sprinkler system, one of us needs to water it soon.

Dave has changed into jogging shorts and is stooped down, tying his shoes, when I step into the bedroom. He watches me while I change, as though I might try to escape.

Listening to our footfalls on a neighborhood road, we trot past houses like ours, many with yards so trim, trees and shrubs so small, it's hard to believe the development is decades old. Multiple cars sit in driveways and at curbside. A shirtless, jeaned Asian teenager washes a silver sedan; a large Hispanic man in a tank shirt, shorts, and flip-flops saws wood in an open garage; three dressed-up Asian women, one holding a white-iced layer cake, laugh and chat by a van with Church of the Good Shepherd painted on its side in English, along with several words in an Asian language.

We jog across Commonwealth Avenue and along a road that goes behind small Fullerton Airport. Railroad tracks are to our right, and large, shaggy lawns are on our left in front of bungalows that predate our housing tract.

"By the way," Dave says, breathing effortlessly, "I had lunch with Mitch from the library, and he said a position's coming open in his department, if you're interested."

"I don't want a library job."

"You hate working for Jane."

"How would you like working for someone who won't speak to you half the time and leaves notes on your desk when you go to the bathroom?"

"So what are you doing about it?"

"What I always do—let her notes lie exactly where she puts them, untouched. It drives her crazy."

"That's no solution."

A single-engine Cessna coasts overhead, the plane's shadow more obtrusive than its sound. The Cessna wobbles, straightens, and touches down on a runway that begins fifty yards in front of us, beyond a ninety-degree bend in the road.

"So, what would you do, Dave, since you know everything?"

"I'd apply for Mitch's job."

"In college I had *shit* library jobs—and *shit* jobs are all you can get in libraries if you're not a librarian. Even my mom says so."

"Maybe get a library degree, like your mom."

"I don't *want* a library degree."

"It would get you out of the bookstore."

"I *like* running the bookstore. I'm my own boss as long as I keep silly-ass Jane out of the way."

"You've bitched about that job for four years, Len. Are you going to bitch about it for the rest of your life?"

I stop running.

Several paces ahead, Dave halts and turns around.

"Thanks for all the support, Dave," I shout. "Everything in this relationship isn't about *me*, you know, even though you think I'm a spoiled fucking brat. I'm not the one who moved across the country for his career. I'm the one who followed *you*. All I have is the best shitty job I could find in this suburban wasteland where we live so you can be near your office and fuck grad students."

I spin around and sprint for home. Dave catches up on his longer legs, but I dart into Commonwealth Avenue. A car brakes, the car behind skids and honks, but I'm already across the street, running on the asphalt shoulder along a wall-height hedge.

I've lost track of Dave by the time I stumble, winded, through the front door of our house. I down two glasses of water at the kitchen sink, shower, and put on a T-shirt and shorts.

Dave leans against the counter, drinking apple juice from a translucent plastic tumbler, when I pad into the kitchen. Shirtless and sweaty in his jogging shorts, he eyes me, gulps more juice, and lowers the tumbler. "You're getting drunk when you're out whoring around, Len—that's why you yell at me all the time when you're home."

"Oh, right. You don't like my temper. You don't like my drinking. You don't like my whoring around. This is déjà vu."

"Only if you want it to be."

"You're so full of shit, Dave. Get fucked."

"I'm tired of being told to get fucked, too."

"You started this. Don't give me your holier-than-thou bullshit. Move out if you don't like what's happening. Get the hell out of my life. I want out of yours."

I storm from the kitchen into the bedroom, grab my wallet off the dresser, and step into my flip-flops. I march out the front door and slam it.

In my car, I don't know where to go.

I turn in the direction of the beach at the Riverside Freeway.

Newport's cool and foggy—Fullerton was eighty degrees and sunny. I carry my flip-flops, kicking across an expanse of dry powder to the ocean and crunch along the tide line, staying high on the slope where the sand is wet and firm. I can taste the salt air and smell beached crustaceans and rotting kelp. The murmur of waves breaking should soothe me but doesn't. I'm cold, goose bumped under my T-shirt.

A man with a handsome chest of gray hair jogs past me. I imagine following him back to his house and going down on him. He looks like a man who thought I was hustling near the Washington Hilton, years ago, and took me to his suite, ordered room service. I danced naked on the bed while he sat in a chair, smoking and watching. I figured I wouldn't take his money. He was good-looking enough that he could have been a TV actor, any of the idols of my boyhood. When he handed me twice as much money as I expected, I thanked him. I was unemployed, and Dave had moved out of our apartment.

Tramping along the surf in light fog, I feel calmer and warmed by the exertion. Cleve could come walking to me up the beach. I started to park near his house but drove on a few blocks, and I'm walking away from where he lives.

I sit in the cool dry sand and try not to think about Dave, or Ian, or Cleve. I feel like walking into the ocean and drowning myself.

By evening, I drive home on surface roads—Coast Highway to Brookhurst. I stop at a taco joint in Anaheim. The place is empty. People eat dinner in restaurants on Saturday night or grill steaks in their backyards with family and friends.

Dave and I don't talk when I get home. I sleep on the unopened sofa bed in the guest room.

He's out most of Sunday, maybe looking at apartments. I hear him come in the back door after I've gone to bed in the guest room again.

❖

On my desk Monday morning is a note paper clipped to an almanac Jane left there while I was at lunch Friday. Over the weekend, she appended a Post-it:

Monsieur Anders, please attend to IMMEDIATELY!!!

She addresses notes to me with the affectation "M. Anders" or "Monsieur Anders"—probably the only college French she remembers. In florid handwriting, on five-by-seven cream stationery embossed "from Jane" at the top, this note rants on both sides of the sheet about books being kept in their proper places. Jane found the almanac in the medical self-help section.

As I'm taking a leak, I decide I'll search online for a writer to invite for a book signing if I can get Jane calmed down enough to not fall apart at the prospect of an author visit.

Strolling back to my office, I'm disappointed to see Jane has arrived. She stands behind her chair, head bowed.

I can't tell whether she's staring at something on her desk or at her note on the almanac on my desk. I sit down and begin searching for books whose authors I might contact.

Jane sits at her desk and shuffles papers on her blotter.

I leave twice to answer questions from Rosie at the register. A third time, I leave to catch a woman in the parking lot who left her wallet on the counter. Walking back indoors, I whistle "Oh, What a Beautiful Morning!" It's afternoon, and I'm about to take off for the gym.

Jane is on her feet, her purse dangling from one hand, her Cadillac keys from the other. This was a short stay, I think. She glares at me as I waltz into the office whistling. She hates whistling. I hope I look as insolent as I feel.

"I've had it with you, Leonard!"

"You've had what with me, Jane?"

"I brought an important matter to your attention, and you have done squat—*absolutely squat!*—about it!"

"Jane, you're like a fly buzzing in peoples' faces, landing on things and producing nothing but annoyance."

She puffs up like an enraged cockatoo, her conical breasts pushing forward in her yellow cashmere sweater. Her red-lips open in an *O*. She presses the pearls I wore naked at her house to her neck with long, vermillion nails. Closing her eyes, she stands trembling.

I see Rosie laughing, wide-eyed, hand over her mouth, twisted around on the stool by the register, looking into our office.

Jane's face contorts, her closed eyelids flutter. Her face looks lopsided. One half doesn't fit the other.

"Jane?"

She doesn't answer.

"Jane, are you all right?"

I walk around our desks and guide her into her chair. I glance through the window at Rosie, who hops off her stool.

"Rosie, come here!"

Rosie hustles into the office. I hold Jane's arm. She can't seem to balance on her chair seat. Rosie leans down to her face.

"Jane, can you open your eyes?" Rosie says. "Jane, can you talk to us?"

I grab the phone on her desk and dial 9-1-1.

In minutes, a fire truck and life-saving van are stopped out front, and eight tall young men and women are inside the store, one of the men asking me questions I can't answer about Jane's medical history, another asking Jane—whose eyes are open now—how many fingers he's holding up.

I ride to the hospital in the front seat of the van and sit in the emergency waiting room until I'm told Jane has been moved to intensive care.

On the fifth floor, in a lobby of blue love seats, I stand at a tinted window with a bird's-eye view of palm trees jutting up between gently sloping low roofs of medical buildings and town homes. A deep male voice speaks behind me.

"Lenny Anders?"

I turn and face a dark-haired youngish man attractive enough that I'd suck his cock in a heartbeat.

"I'm Chip Morris, Jane's son."

His handshake is firm. He smiles when I say, "You're the Santa Barbara one."

"I'm the Los Angeles one. I've talked to the doctor, and he says my mother had a minor stroke. They'll keep her in intensive care overnight and watch her in the hospital another day or two, but she should be all right. She was able to talk to me."

I burst out laughing. "Frankly, your mother scared the shit out of me."

Chip laughs and lays a hand on my shoulder. "Thanks for coming to the hospital with her. You can go if you want, now that I'm here. In fact, when the doctor mentioned you were in the waiting room, Mom said, 'Who's minding the store?'"

"Did she really?" I'm giggly with relief. "I'll go mind the store."

I hold out my hand for Chip to shake again, and I give him a hug he doesn't expect.

Rosie's behind the register, missing her afternoon class, as I pay my cab driver and hustle into the bookstore.

"Jane's all right," I yell and walk, laughing, up to the counter. "Her son, Chip, is with her. A minor stroke. They'll keep her in the hospital a couple of days."

"Oh, *querido*, a close call."

Rosie bites her lip. She starts laughing with me. She laughs harder and harder. "I know I shouldn't laugh," she splutters, "but you were *so* funny! 'Jane, you are like a fly buzzing in peoples' faces!' Oh, my God!" Mascara-streaked tears run down Rosie's cheeks. She shakes her head and wags an index finger at me. "Too close a call, *querido*. You and Jane are like oil and water."

"I know. I need to get out of this place. Especially with you leaving. I don't want to be here without you."

I wrap my arms around Rosie and hold her tight, swaying our bodies side to side, until I feel her tense up. Her smiling eyes stare at me in wonder after I let go.

"What did I feel in your pocket, *querido*?"

"Dave and I had a fight, so I haven't been getting much lately."

"Oh, no! My lovebirds aren't cooing?"

"We're cooing, sort of. Dave's tired of my complaints about Jane. I take her bitching all day, and he gets pissy because I come home and talk about it."

"Oh, *querido*, I had a similar experience with Alan when I was living with my self-destructive friend, Christa. I got mad at Alan's impatience, but then we talked about his feelings, and I understood how exasperated my horror stories made him. Because I was experiencing Christa and not just hearing about her, I was able to tolerate her lying and stealing and sleeping with crackheads. Going through something awful, you cope. If you just hear about it, you can't understand why anyone would put up with it. Don't be mad at Dave, *querido*."

"We'll see. Thanks for staying this afternoon."

"Honey would have stayed, too, but she had an exam."

Rosie takes her book bag from under the counter as Ian waltzes in the front door. They both head for the time clock.

I ring up three spy novels for a man in a sweat suit while two women browse greeting cards near the front of the store.

"Rosie said Jane's in the hospital?" Ian says, coming around the counter.

"She had a minor stroke."

I tell him the story, downplaying the fact that Jane and I were arguing when she had her stroke.

"Wait till she hears you're leaving," Ian says. "She'd better be on tranquilizers."

Standing in front of me, he rises up and down on the balls of his feet, flapping his arms like he's trying to fly. I grab his wrists and root him to the floor.

"Stop bouncing. You're making me more nervous than I already am."

"I bought my ticket for Baltimore. I would have texted you, but I was afraid Dave might see it." He hands me a scrap of paper with an airline, a flight number, and a date on it. "You should go online right now. It's not cheap, but this close to time to go, it won't get cheaper."

I gaze at the parking lot. Rosie smiles, backing out the front door.

Ian cracks his knuckles.

"We could drive to Baltimore," I suggest.

"Would you want to drive that far?"

"Probably not."

"I'll buy a car there."

I nod a few times.

"You don't have to do anything you don't want to do, Lenny."

"Some people would say I haven't done anything I didn't want to do in my whole life."

I squeeze his shoulders and mosey into my office. I've had several cups of coffee, nothing to eat but an egg salad sandwich in the hospital cafeteria, and no midday workout. I'm jittery and hungry.

When I leave the bookstore, Ian's with a customer. I nod good night.

In my car, I use my cell to find the flight Ian will be on. The refundable fares are absurdly high. I close the site without buying a ticket.

Dave's washing lettuce at the sink when I come in. We glance at each other. He dries his hands on a dish towel, and I take a beer from the refrigerator. "I didn't expect to find you home," I say.

"Where'd you expect me to be?"

"I don't know. Where were you all day yesterday?"

"Working at my office."

"I thought maybe you were looking at apartments."

"Is that what you want me to do?"

"No. You moved out last time. I'll move out this time."

I change into jeans and a red shirt I leave unbuttoned. I sit on our high double bed, legs folded, and massage the balls of my feet while I gaze into the fabric of the green comforter as though expecting magic words of instruction to appear. When Dave and I split up in Washington, we'd lived together less than a year in a furnished apartment. He packed his clothes and books in an afternoon and left.

I don't know how to begin to move out. I don't even know how to pay for my Baltimore ticket. Our checking account is joint, our savings account joint, our credit cards. We own our house together, our cars. We never spend money without telling each other.

I hear the back door open and close. Dave's car idles in the alley and drives away.

The lettuce Dave was washing is on the sink counter, along with two bowls, two plates, two knives, two forks, two cans of chili, and a box of rice.

He isn't home when I go to bed or when I leave for work in the morning. I text him after lunch, but he doesn't reply. I phone, and he answers, hears my voice, and cuts the call off.

I'm with a supervisor from the bookstore's cleaning service when Ian arrives. By the time I'm free, Ian's helping a man on crutches, leg in a cast, list of books in hand. Ian and I glance at each other like kids wanting to go out and play.

"I'll see you tonight, if it's all right, Ian?" I call.

"Sure."

I lock my office and walk out to my car. After loosening my tie, I find Ian's flight on my cell. A young man walks out of a discount clothing boutique in the strip mall and heads across the lot toward me. I watch him. He isn't good-looking enough that he'd be of particular interest to me if he weren't staring at me. For a moment I think he's about to walk up to my car, but he gets into one facing mine. He begins looking at his phone but glances at me every few seconds. I go to a hookup site I've heard of, quickly register, and search to see if anyone near me is on it. Someone is. I pull off my tie, unbutton my shirt, and open it wide.

He finds me. *r u in car w shirt open?*

Yes. Join me.

He gets out of his car and appears uncertain. I reach across my passenger seat and shove the door open. He climbs in. He wears a wedding ring. So do I, of course. I suspect this guy has a wife, maybe children. I drive across Harbor Boulevard and circle blocks in the neighborhood while my new friend kneels on the floor on the passenger side and does me. He keeps my spent cock in his mouth while he squirts, politely trying not to make a mess. "Don't worry," I tell him. "I like cum." He uses his handkerchief to clean up and resumes his seat.

I park where I was. Without either of us mentioning meeting again, he gets out of my car and into his. After he drives off, I walk across the lot to the Tap Room.

I leave the bar three hours later. Dave would shit if he saw me getting into my car after as much as I drank.

I burp McDonald's food as Ian lets me into his house. I nudge the door closed with my shoe heel and take him in my arms. The ten o'clock news blares on the TV in his new-smelling living room. I kiss him, walk to the kitchen, and lean against the counter while I pull my phone from my pants pocket and call home.

Dave answers. "Hello?…Lenny, is that you? Hello?"

Fuck you for cutting me off this afternoon, I planned to say. But I power off without speaking.

"Who were you calling?"

"No one. Don't worry about it."

I walk over and lower the TV volume to stop the speaker from jarring. I don't know why Ian plays the TV so loud, except maybe his mother did, because I remember it blaring the night I helped get her to bed.

"Take off your clothes, Ian. I want to hold your naked ass in my arms."

"You're drunk."

"Come on. I want to hold your naked ass." I'm slurring my words.

"You're lucky a cop didn't stop you, Lenny."

"God damn it, I'm so in love with you."

He pulls off his T-shirt, shrugs out of his jeans and briefs, and steps into my arms. I tuck his curved erection between my pant legs and squeeze. We maneuver into his bedroom with him standing on the toes of my shoes.

A plane ticket printout lies on his cardboard dresser.

"First thing tomorrow," I mumble.

"First thing, what?"

I shake my head. "Something at the store."

Ian helps me undress, and we lie on his bed kissing until he slides down. Only I'm too drunk, and I fall asleep.

I make it up to him in the morning. I ball his belly while we hold each other's cocks between our bodies. I make him moan and swear, the way I love to.

After opening the bookstore under a gray sky, I leave Mai-Ly behind the register and sit at my desk using my cell to buy a ticket on Ian's flight. I replace Dave's cell number with mine and select phone as my preferred method of contact, so they won't message the email address Dave and I normally use when buying anything. I'm the one who goes online and pays our credit card bill, so Dave won't see the charge. By the time the bill comes, he'll know anyhow.

❖

Instead of going to the gym on lunch hour, I drive around East Fullerton.

Parked on a side street with my seatback reclined halfway, I stare at the car ceiling, ready to skip over the whole five weeks before Ian and I go to Baltimore. I masturbate surreptitiously, imagining the guy from yesterday blowing me again.

❖

Dave, in a white T-shirt and dark blue sweats, leans against the kitchen counter doing nothing apparent as I come in the back door from work. We look at each other without speaking. He watches me unbutton my dress shirt.

"Where were you last night, Lenny?"

"With Cleve, not that it's your business."

"Why are you lying to me?" he says.

"Don't call me a liar."

"Then don't lie to me."

"I like Cleve. We get drunk together."

Dave tucks his hands down the front of his sweatpants and absently fondles himself, something he does around the house. "The bank called because someone in Chicago tried to use a fake credit card with my name and number. So, the lady read me other recent charges, and there was this airline ticket I said wasn't ours. But she called back and said the purchase was made from guess what cell number? Are you going anywhere you want to tell me about, Len? Like maybe to Baltimore?"

"The ticket is for Jane." I haven't told him that Jane is in the hospital.

"Bullshit, Lenny. You're such a liar." Looking disgusted, Dave turns to the sink.

I change into a T-shirt and shorts. The sunless evening tints our unmade bed and the clothes strewn on the floor blue.

From the hall, I lean into Dave's den. He sits at his desk. "Jane's going to see her friend from college again—the woman she visited in Annapolis. She can't do anything for herself, especially online." I don't want to lie to Dave but can't bring myself to tell him the truth. Without looking up, he pencils a note in the margin of a research journal open on his desk. When I'm in the hall on my way to the kitchen, he says, "You really are a *case*, Len."

We snack separately for dinner. I sleep on the unopened sofa bed.

In morning light, drowsing to a mixture of news and static on the guest room clock radio, I hear Dave go out the back door. He's early.

Tall, plump, hoary Jack—of all people—is at the bookstore with Mai-Ly when I arrive. I haven't seen Jack since Ian's mother's funeral. He wears the orange cardigan he kept at the store and wore for the five years I worked with him and for several years before, according to Jane, who hates the sweater. Jack smiles at me from behind metal-framed bifocals.

"I knew you'd be along," he says.

"What brings you here, Jack?"

"Jane called from the hospital yesterday and asked me to come in. I told her I didn't think it was necessary."

"She's so crazy, Jack. If I don't get away from that woman,

I'll be the next to have a stroke. How long did she ask you to work?"

"I told her I'd come in today, and we'd see if you thought you'd need me other days. She was worried about the store being short one person."

"Short one person? It's not like she does anything here."

"I didn't want to upset her."

"She goes away on vacations and we survive."

"I can watch the register for a few hours and tell her we talked, you'll call if you need me."

I shake my head in disbelief. "Thanks, Jack."

At the gym, Tony sits on a bench in a sweat-soaked tank shirt and trunks. He holds one shoe, wears the other. I toss my shower towel in a bin. The humid locker room smells like used bath water.

"Lost in thought, Tony?"

He glances sideways, up at me, as I open my locker. I step into my underpants, pull them to my waist and sit on the bench beside him. "Something the matter?" I ask.

"I'm fucked, that's all. I screwed Cyndi. I've screwed her a few times. I don't know whether I feel better or worse. I don't know what I feel. I was fucked before, I'm fucked now."

"Cyndi's the woman whose husband left her with the one-year-old?"

Tony nods and drops the shoe he's holding, takes off his other gym shoe and one sock.

"She's all I can think about. When I'm in bed with Tess, Tess is Cyndi. Do you know how that feels?"

"Give it a little time. Let your head clear—both your heads."

"The good news is I'm being transferred to Seattle." Tony takes off his other sock and sits with his heel resting on the edge of the bench.

I stand up, pull on my trousers, and buckle my belt. "I'm transferring to Baltimore. Transferring myself, that is. The only place Royal Books could transfer me is to the hard luck line when the place goes belly-up."

"Cyndi will be a thousand miles away. Maybe I can make a clean start."

"Maybe you can."

I slip into my shirt and button it. "Do you want to have a cup of coffee after you shower, talk a little?"

"I'm already late getting back to work. I don't want to screw up there. Work is the one thing in my life going right."

Tony rolls off his gym shorts and jock strap in a wad, wraps a towel around his waist, and pads to the showers. I watch his handsome back disappear before I finish dressing.

At a drive-through waiting for a roast beef sandwich, I have a fantasy in which I cure Tony of his female worries.

I'd like to go somewhere and suck a whole line of big dicks, I realize. The thought depresses me. I'm regressing, not settling down with age.

I feel a glimmer more cheerful walking into the bookstore and seeing my office door closed, physical evidence Jane's out of my hair. Then I think of her stroke and feel guilty. As I stroll across the floor carrying a large coffee from the doughnut shop, I watch Mai-Ly at the cash register hold the phone receiver over the counter. "A call for you, Lenny."

"Lenny Anders. May I help you?"

"Hello," Cleve says.

I'm so surprised it takes me a second to say hello back.

"I'm home from New Zealand. Your message said to call."

It takes me another moment to remember I called Cleve

from Jane's house while Ian was in the shower. "Let me go to my office, Cleve." I settle in my chair. Mai-Ly, watching through the glass, hangs up the phone at the counter. "So, how was New Zealand?"

Cleve tells me about his trip, while I prod him with questions and ignore his waning enthusiasm for answering them. I ask what he liked most.

"I don't know. All of it, whatever. I just called while I had a chance. I'll be up at Big Bear for the weekend and then in Arizona for most of next week."

"Are the same guys you told me about going up to Big Bear?"

"More or less."

"Sounds like fun. Skiing, I guess?"

"In *May*?" He's silent, then adds quietly, "We sit in the hot tub and drink whiskey. I should get back to work. I have a lot to do."

"Could I go up to Big Bear with you?"

"That's not why I called."

I glimpse Mai-Ly, looking over her shoulder at me as a customer stands on the other side of the counter. I swivel so my back is to them.

Cleve sighs. We're both silent.

"We're just talking about a weekend, right?" I say. "A hot tub, a little whiskey. Bed, if you want."

"If you're serious, how early could you leave tomorrow?"

"Four o'clock?"

"I could pick you up at the bookstore on my way."

Mai-Ly's in my doorway. "Lenny, I have an over-ring."

"I'll be right there, sweetie. Four tomorrow, then, Cleve?"

"Sure." He laughs. "You're full of surprises, Lenny."

As I clear Mai-Ly's over-ring, I realize Saturday will be the seventh anniversary of my first date with Dave. I wonder if unconsciously I knew I'd want to be elsewhere for the day. How do you spend an anniversary if you're about to split up? I also wonder where I'll tell Ian I'm going for the weekend, if I need to tell him anything.

Instead of returning to my desk, I wander into the travel aisle and pick up an Eastern US travel guide, flipping to the section about Baltimore. I miss living in the East, miss being in a walkable city with street life, miss hot summers with thunderstorms. I remember waiting out a downpour with Dave under a portico, near our Washington apartment. We'd been in bed all day and were on our way out to eat when the sky opened up.

Ian arrives at five, and I mention I'm leaving early tomorrow. "Dave and I are going to Palm Springs for a weekend we planned a while ago. I didn't want to make a big deal of it by canceling."

Ian shrugs, and I head into my office. He doesn't follow.

As I lock my door for the day, Ian keeps an eye on the register while he helps Mai-Ly tag sci-fi books. He's talking about James Joyce. I wave as I walk around the counter, and Mai-Ly waves back. Ian nods in my direction and keeps talking.

At home, I tell Dave I'm going to Big Bear with Cleve, leaving from work tomorrow. He lifts a teabag out of his Georgetown mug and watches it twirl on its string.

I grab a backpack I used as a book bag in college off the closet floor. I stuff underwear, socks, jeans, and a sweatshirt into it. Remembering there'll be a hot tub, I add an Australian swimsuit I can wear like a thong. I imagine drinking whiskey with a group of guys in steamy air under a starry mountain sky.

Dave and I spend the evening and night in separate rooms.

As I'm about to leave the house in the gray of another overcast morning, I can't find my phone. "Have you seen my cell anywhere?" I ask Dave. He wallows on the unmade double bed I haven't slept in for a week. He's wearing the same dark blue sweats and armpit-stained dingy white T-shirt he's worn around the house for several days. His arms are raised, his hands locked behind his head, his hair in need of a shower. As I stare into the dim room from the doorway, I smell sweat and semen on the sheets. Neither of us has done laundry lately. "Shouldn't you be getting ready for school?"

"My morning class isn't meeting today. They needed time for field work. Say hi to Ian for me." Dave's light blue eyes focus past me, on the hallway wall at my back. "Len, do you remember telling me I was infatuated with him and it would pass?"

Dave reminds me of patients who stared out of their rooms when my mom and I visited my father in mental hospitals.

"I must have left my phone at work," I say. "See you Sunday."

7. A HARD DOG TO KEEP ON THE PORCH

Cleve pulls between two luxury SUVs on a gravel driveway. A motorcycle sits on the other side of one. Both SUVs and the bike are nosed up to a bungalow otherwise surrounded by tall spruce trees, branchless at their bottoms. I climb out and stand in the gravel listening to a car pass on the road at my back while Cleve crunches around to open the trunk. We step inside into a front room with a stone fireplace, a wood-armed sofa with matching chairs, and a brown oval rug over red linoleum. Glancing through a doorway, I see a leather jacket and a helmet on a bed covered by a blanket of bright bleeding colors.

"My friend Lyle rides the motorcycle," Cleve says. "I should have warned you Don keeps the house furnished as a weekend rental."

"I like it."

We drop our bags in a room with a small window looking out to the driveway and another out to the trees. I follow Cleve back through the front room into the kitchen, where an old oak table has eight chairs around it. The frames of the glass-windowed cabinets are thick with white paint. I smell clam chowder simmering in a large uncovered pot.

We cross a threshold from red linoleum to coarse-textured gray carpet, and we're in a much newer, pine-paneled room with an open-beam ceiling. A king-sized bed and a love seat sit sideways to a sliding glass door leading to a deck on which three men with goblets of wine stand talking and laughing. Forty or so yards down a gentle slope, Big Bear Lake glimmers in the twilight.

As we step outside, I recognize chubby white-haired Don, Cleve's housemate. Smiling, Don shakes my hand and introduces me to Thaddeus, a tall, black man of Don's soft, fleshy build, with graying temples and large, watery eyes framed by tortoiseshell glasses. Thaddeus is a studio accountant, Cleve told me on the drive up. Cleve also told me Thaddeus and Don were lovers for several years, as Cleve and Don were a long time ago.

Cleve introduces me to his friend Lyle. Staring at Lyle's handsome shaved head, I have no trouble imagining Cleve and Lyle as ex-tricks. Lyle is fortyish and chesty, with muscular, tattooed arms in a sleeveless black sweatshirt. While he looks me over with phlegmatic gray eyes, I picture his motorcycle between his legs.

Don motions at the lake with his wineglass. "We're observing Edsel pitching woo to his young friend."

Don and Thaddeus chuckle. Lyle, Cleve, and I smile and look down the slope at the backs of two men in jeans and jackets standing on a log at lakeside. One of the men, with scraggly hair around a bald spot, has his arm around the other, with a solid mop of blond hair.

Cleve puts his arm around me. "I want to get out of my suit."

"I'll change into jeans," I say. We go inside. I glance along the deck and see the hot tub, near another sliding glass door.

Cleve takes two wineglasses from a kitchen cabinet and

fills them, emptying one of a few open bottles standing on the counter. "To the weekend." We touch glasses.

Lyle comes in from the deck and sets his empty glass on the table. "I'm going to catch a few winks before dinner."

"I love a Friday evening nap," Cleve says.

Cleve and I follow Lyle to our adjacent doors, where Lyle disappears behind his as it closes.

"We'd be in the other bedroom off the deck," Cleve says quietly, as he closes our door, "only Don promised it to Edsel in case the college kid he brought wants to try more than kissing."

"I want to try more than kissing." I unbutton Cleve's dress shirt and thread my fingers into his chest hair.

"Where'd you tell Dave you were going this weekend?"

"To Big Bear, with you. You like that, don't you?"

"I do."

We undress each other as we kiss.

On our bed, I nudge Cleve onto his back and kneel over him. Our metal headboard wobbles and taps the wall between our room and Lyle's as I move my lips up and down on Cleve's thick shaft and its plum.

❖

In T-shirts, jeans, and bare feet, we join the others in the kitchen, Cleve's arm around my waist. There are smiles. My hair is seriously mussed. I started to comb it, but Cleve said he liked it that way.

"Are we hungry or did we just eat something?" Don says as he stirs the clam chowder.

I grin as Cleve beams. Cleve pushes through a door across from the dining table, into a bathroom. I glimpse a claw-footed tub and a clear shower curtain on metal rings.

Moving close to Lyle, I ask if he got his nap.

"More or less," he says, avoiding my eyes. He turns to a platter of broccoli and dip on the countertop as Don hands me a glass of wine.

Cleve comes out of the bathroom, and I step in.

When I come out, two more men are in the kitchen. "Lenny, this is Edsel and Jason," Don says.

Edsel, the man with scraggly hair around a bald spot, shakes my hand while he strokes his goatee. His shoulders droop, and his bowling-ball belly puffs out his plaid shirt. His friendly, squinting eyes meet mine and turn with pride to Jason.

Blond Jason, with blue eyes and thick lips, is a small muscle boy packed into a long-sleeved thermal undershirt and pale jeans with the knees out. He laughs and blushes when Edsel and I look at him.

❖

After supper and several bottles of wine, Cleve and Thaddeus help Don load bowls and plates into a portable dishwasher they roll a few feet out from the wall. Cleve sets brandy snifters on the table, while Don and Thaddeus talk at the sink. Thaddeus disappears into the bedroom Cleve and I walked through on our way to the balcony earlier.

"His back's bothering him," Don says to the five of us at the table. He picks up two snifters of brandy. "I'd better go help him with the new massaging shower nozzle. He's great with numbers and crossword puzzles, but all thumbs with contraptions." Don rolls his eyes and saunters into the bedroom.

Edsel, squinting, his face in a grin, whispers in muscle boy Jason's ear. Jason gets up from the table, opens a door next to the bathroom, and steps into a pantry-sized cubbyhole where he picks up a jacket from a cot. He and Edsel carry their brandy snifters to the second back bedroom.

Cleve suggests some air. Taking our snifters and the brandy bottle, he, Lyle, and I grab shoes and jackets from our bedrooms and head out the front door to the gravel driveway. A few cars pass on the road at our backs as we crunch around the side of the house to needle-matted earth. The air smells of damp wood and moss. From between clouds, a full moon shines on the lake. A small boat moves away from shore, its oars lapping the water. We hear Jason laugh, while the glowing tip of a cigarette wags from Edsel's mouth as he rows.

Cleve and I settle on a log several yards from the lake. Lyle wanders nearer the water, bends over, straightens up, and pitches a stone into the depth. He picks up another stone and pitches it, and another.

"Come sit with us." Cleve pats our log.

"Actually, I'm tired," Lyle says, walking over to us. Cleve picks up the brandy bottle from the ground and refreshes Lyle's snifter.

"Thanks. I'm heading in. Good night, guys."

"See you in the morning," Cleve says.

Lyle and I exchange good-night glances, our eyes loaded with interest in each other.

Cleve tightens his arm around my waist as Lyle's footfalls fade behind us. The night is cold, the seat of my jeans damp from the log. I can see my breath as Cleve kisses my temple. "There's so much like this we can do," he says.

"Sure."

I sip and swallow. Edsel and Jason's boat is motionless. Their words reach us as murmurs across the water.

"Your friend Lyle seems like a nice guy. Why didn't you and he—?"

Cleve lets my question drift out over the lake.

"Lyle and I slept together twice," he says. "We weren't each other's type. He's my dentist, so that's how we met."

I nod. A match flares as Edsel lights another cigarette. The boat begins to move.

We undress in our room, and I stop Cleve with just his shirt off and rub my hands in his chest hair. "I haven't been on my knees for you, Cleve."

He pulls off his shoes and socks, and I undo and lower his jeans, tugging them off over each foot while he stands on the other. Kneeling on a throw rug, I watch his chest swell with manly pride until my mouth fills with cum.

I ask Cleve to go to the breakfast table shirtless the next morning, and he does even though the house is cold. The guys seem to understand. I make plain that I like looking at him.

❖

In a sweater shop on nearby Lake Arrowhead, Don and Cleve chat with the owner, while Thaddeus and Edsel step outside with cigarettes ready to light. The afternoon's gray. Thaddeus leans on the rail, looking across the narrow lake at a condominium development. Edsel faces in, stroking his chin whiskers and keeping a squinty eye on muscle boy Jason, who looks through a rack of flannel shirts with me. Lyle stands by a sweater table at the end of the shirt rack. I watch him hold up a bulky knit pullover. "You'd look good in that," I say.

"So would you."

I take a rust-colored shirt off the rod and hold it in front of myself. "What do you think, Jason?"

"Nice." He laughs, like a motor running.

"Are you and Edsel a hot item?"

"Edsel's an interesting man. He owns a used book store in Hollywood. You work in a bookstore, don't you?"

"Royal Books, in Fullerton. You're a sophomore at Pepperdine?"

Jason nods. "I've been in Royal Books. I have an aunt in La Habra."

"Do you live on campus?"

"I live at home, in Oxnard."

"Are you enjoying a weekend with the boys?"

He laughs and blushes. He's even cuter red-faced.

"Did you bring a swimsuit in case we crank up the hot tub tonight?" I ask.

"We will," Lyle says, at my back. "It's a Saturday night ritual."

"Hear that, Jason? You're going to be in a ritual."

Jason tries to hide his flushed face by looking through more shirts.

Lyle frowns and goes outside to join Thaddeus and Edsel. Lyle's back looks good in a leather jacket and jeans.

At the house, I ask Cleve if I can make a call on his phone. I carry it out to the driveway for privacy, and reach Dave's message center. "I just called to see how you are." I don't mention today is our anniversary. "I'm on Cleve's phone. Mine wasn't at the bookstore. Well..." I wait in case Dave might answer. "See you tomorrow."

I cry in the shower before dinner. On our first date, Dave and I danced to Stevie Wonder's "I Just Called to Say I Love You." After we'd dated for nearly a year, lived together for a little more than that, and been separated for a little less, Dave was in California, and I still in Washington. He called on the third anniversary of our first date and sang the chorus of that song instead of saying hello. The conversation got us back together. I came to California within the month. On our three anniversaries since, we've danced to Stevie Wonder.

The hot tub feels anticlimactic by the time our group sinks into its froth with after-dinner glasses of whiskey at hand. Don and Thaddeus are indoors. Cleve and I wear swimsuits. Scraggly-bearded Edsel, with his concave chest and convex belly, stands nude on the deck before immersing himself. Slurring his words, he asks Lyle, Cleve, and me if Jason isn't the sweetest kid we've ever seen. Jason, in red surfer baggies, is busy controlling Edsel's hands underwater.

Lyle lifts his upper body above the churning surface, the gray waistband of his black briefs just above the foam. His shaved head sweats. While he looks with disgust at Edsel, I study the nubs of his hard nipples. I could make his chest feel so good.

Cleve finds my hand and holds it.

Jason says he's going indoors and climbs out of the tub. Edsel stumbles up onto the deck and tries to help Jason towel off, but Jason steps out of his reach. Edsel teeters backward and falls into the tub, landing in Cleve's arms. Edsel lies giggling up at Cleve. Cleve grins at Lyle and me. I hop out and help hoist Edsel back on the deck and steady him on his feet.

Jason steps through the doorway to Edsel's room. Edsel waddles his dripping, saggy bare ass after Jason, but Jason walks through the bedroom to the kitchen. Edsel picks up a pair of striped lounging pants, gets one leg into them, and topples on the bed with his other leg raised. He reminds me of a bug on its back.

"Are things all right in there?" Cleve says, smiling up as I stand looking inside.

"More or less." I grin and resettle in the water.

Cleve reaches behind himself for the whiskey bottle, refills our glasses, and hands mine to me. Cupping its heavy hexagonal shape, I sip and sink deeper under the froth, tipping back my head to look for stars in the cloud-covered sky.

By the time Cleve, Lyle, and I climb out of the hot tub and towel dry, we're too overheated and drunk to feel cold, although the needle of a round thermometer mounted against the house points to thirty-nine degrees. Cleve turns off the power to the hot tub.

Edsel's bedroom is dark, and his drape closed. A lamp shines in Don and Thaddeus's room, so we troop along the deck and step in through their door. Thaddeus is asleep. Don, in a paisley robe, sits on the love seat reading a biography that sells well even in Royal Books. An open door looks into a turquoise-tiled bathroom with a turquoise tub and a massive showerhead. Cleve drops our towels into a hamper in there. Whispering good night, we file through to the kitchen.

I see light under the closed door to the pantry where Jason's cot is. Cleve steps into the bathroom, next to Jason's cubbyhole. Lyle follows me into the living room, our moist feet squeaking on the linoleum.

I stop outside the room Cleve and I share, and Lyle stops outside his room. As I take a swallow of whiskey, Lyle takes a deep breath and faces me. I glance at his black underwear and see the outline of his erection.

"I like your swimsuit, Lyle."

"I like yours."

"It's Australian, the kind lifeguards wear."

I pull my suit into my crack and turn my backside to him. He caresses my buttocks. His chest presses my shoulder blades. He reaches around to my stomach and pulls me tighter against him. Through his wet underwear, I feel the length of his bone vertically between my buns.

"Maybe you could sleep with Cleve and me."

"Cleve wouldn't go for it."

We hear the toilet flush in the bath off the kitchen. Lyle fills my navel with a fingertip while he puts his other hand down the front of my trunks. His thumb lies along my shaft. He presses the tip of his index finger against my dick hole and makes tiny circles around its slippery rim.

"I like your finger there."

"So do I."

Cleve's footfalls pat on the kitchen linoleum, and Lyle lets go of me, ducks into his room, and shuts the door.

I step into our room, flip on the light, and ease the door part closed with my heel. I leave my swimsuit in my crack and lie on my belly.

Cleve slips through the door at my back and stops. He climbs on the bed and kisses his way down my spine to my buttocks. He kisses my cheeks. He pushes them together with his fingers, edges them apart with his thumbs. He eases my swimsuit out of my crack, pulls it down my legs and off, over my feet. He fingers my heels, traces his way along my insteps to finger the balls of my feet and my toes. I lift the side of my face from my pillow and stare at him kneeling upright on the foot of the bed.

Muscular thighs, stout hard cock, flat belly as hirsute as his chest, pecs swollen from adrenaline. Nipples sharp as jewels cut through curly dark hair. Straddling one of my legs, he scoots on his knees up to my butt, lubricates my hole and sheathes himself, then mounts me. He rolls us on our sides and strokes my cock with one hand, tweaking my nipples with the other while he moves in and out. I come as I squeeze my ring with all its strength around his husky shaft. He breathes, "I love you so much," and follows me into orgasm.

As we lie spooning in our exhaustion, I wish he hadn't said he loves me. But I know it's easy to say when you're about to come.

Cleve rises to his feet, removes his condom, and wraps it in a Kleenex. He tugs open a small wood-framed window, crooked on its rope sash. Cold air flows in.

I listen for sounds from Lyle's silent room. Our headboard tapped the wall as Cleve's thrusts became frantic. As though reading my mind, Cleve stands still and glances at the wall between the two rooms and grins. He lies back down.

I pick my whiskey glass up off the floor, tilt it, and sip. I snuggle my butt against Cleve's crotch and use his solid upper arm as a pillow. He pulls up the blanket. He talks about how much he loves mountains and about wanting to take me to the Tetons. I fall asleep half-listening.

Waking in the dark, I sense the whiskey glass tipped over in my hand. Cleve's on his other side, turned away from me, breathing evenly. I finger the sheet near the lip of the glass and feel a small damp spot.

My head aches, and I need to pee. My mouth is dry as sand. I pull the door closed as I leave. The house is silent, except for Lyle quietly snoring behind his door. Through the black living room windowpanes, evergreen trunks are just visible in the cloudy moonlight, straight and bare like giant pegs. I'm awake, drunk, cold.

I pad into the kitchen, into the bathroom, and pee by the faint glow seeping through a window above the tub. I don't flush because I don't want to make more noise.

I cross the kitchen to the sink, fill a glass with water, and gulp it while staring out into the woods. A dim light flickers on behind me. I turn. Jason's door is ajar.

Setting my glass on the counter, I step into the middle of the kitchen. A small cone-shaped green lamp hangs by a cord from the ceiling above Jason's cot and spotlights him, naked on his back atop disheveled covers. With his hands under his head, pink soles of his feet toward me, he stares down his body in my direction. From my vantage point, his biceps and pecs look like a mountain range on the horizon. His toes wiggle, and his erection wags across his smooth belly. I enter and ease the door closed. He scoots over on the narrow mattress and rolls on his side. I lie down and gather his compact bulk in my arms.

"Edsel's right. You are the sweetest kid in the world."

Jason laughs. I smile and kiss him.

"I'm going to tell you something," I say, moving my hand from his thigh to his ass. "Do you feel where my finger is?"

He laughs again.

"Don't ever let anyone in there unless he has a condom on. Unless he has *two* condoms on."

"You're drunk."

"Do you hear me? Because every gay man you meet is going to want in there."

"I know about AIDS. I've had sex before. Sixty-nined, at least. Edsel doesn't know or he wouldn't leave me alone."

"Don't be too hard on Edsel. You're a bundle of muscle to resist."

"So are you."

Pinned between me and the wall, Jason squirms down along the cot. I grip his scalp, through its lush hair, as I pump in and out of his mouth.

He keeps sucking on my balls after I come. His muscled calves and feet stick off the cot and thrash while he beats off.

As we cuddle, I run my fingers through his hair, feeling its softness. My own hair is still full enough that I can shake my head after a shower, and it falls into place. But my hairline isn't as low on my forehead as it once was.

"I should get out of here, champ," I whisper. "Edsel and Cleve wouldn't be happy if they caught us in bed."

Jason laughs. I squeeze him and lay my head on the pillow

we share. We drape our arms over each other's hips. In the light of the weak bulb hanging above us, I watch his blue irises disappear behind heavy lids. The tips of our noses touch, and I feel my own eyelids growing heavy.

The next thing I'm conscious of are voices in the kitchen. Lying on my back, I rise on my elbows. Jason lies asleep half on top of me, an arm thrown over my chest, a leg folded over my thigh. The head of his boner nudges the head of mine. Daylight gleams under the door of our windowless cell, while the bulb above us adds its weak wattage. I hear knives and forks scraping plates, hear mugs and glasses thumping the kitchen table. Edsel, Cleve, and Lyle talk about a rumor that a young leading man is having an affair with a male porn star.

I lift up on my elbows. Jason wakes.

"Here come more eggs," Don says. "More eggs, Edsel?"

"No, thanks. I probably should wake Jason."

"Leave the boy alone. The young need their sleep."

"Good morning, gentlemen." Thaddeus's voice.

"You were in the shower, Thaddeus?" Cleve asks.

"We're not allowed to the breakfast table until we've showered?" Thaddeus replies jocularly.

"I mean, is Lenny using your shower?"

"Don't I wish?"

"I guess he went for a walk."

"If he went to the right, the guys around the curve will feast on his bones and leave nothing but a hair or an eyelash. He does have the most beautiful eyelashes. So bedroomy."

"Sit down, Thaddeus," Don says. "Have eggs while they're warm. Have more eggs, Lyle, Cleve."

In our cell, Jason grins at me. "You do have beautiful eyelashes."

"I'm a fuckin' prince. We're in deep shit, my young friend."

"What's the worst they can do to us?"

"You'll be okay. You could get by with anything."

"Maybe if you wait, they'll all go to their rooms or go out somewhere."

I brush Jason's hair to the side of his forehead and kiss him.

"Where's your boy Jason this morning, Edsel?" Thaddeus says.

"I'm going to wake him."

"Let him be," Don says.

A chair scrapes linoleum, and Jason and I freeze. Knuckles rap on our door.

"Jason? Breakfast is on the table. Are you awake in there?"

The door opens a crack, and Edsel sees us. The door coasts farther open. Edsel steps back. His eyes reduce to slivers. His jaw trembles.

I stand up and step out of the small room, pulling the door shut behind me. Cleve, Lyle, and Thaddeus stop eating. Don glances from the stove and quickly turns back to the skillet. Edsel stamps from the kitchen into his bedroom.

"Morning," I say. I and my flagging erection go to the bedroom where my clothes lie on the floor.

After dressing, I walk back to the kitchen. Cleve, Lyle, and Thaddeus eat in silence. Don is gone. I slip into the bathroom and shut the door, pee and wash my face.

When I open the door, Cleve's chair is empty. I wonder if I should help myself to coffee from a pot on the stove.

Thaddeus avoids my eyes, getting up and carrying his plate to a stack of other dirty plates on the sink counter. Lyle follows and adds his dishes to the stack. Thaddeus goes to the back of the house, Lyle the front.

I sit at one of two clean place settings, scoop eggs on a

plate and take a muffin. I don't think my stomach can handle bacon. I eat staring at my food until I see two puffy pink hands gripping a chair back across the table from me. Don almost smiles.

"You may find it hard to believe," he says quietly, "but I was once quite a catch and couldn't behave myself either."

Thaddeus walks into the kitchen, and Don quickly steps away from the table. Thaddeus points to the bedroom with his thumb. "Could you show me how to adjust that darn showerhead again, Don?"

"But of course, dear heart."

As soon as they leave the room, the door to Jason's cubbyhole opens and he emerges, half-naked, in knee-less jeans. He looks at me and laughs. "Man, you look popular. I'm getting my butt in the shower before someone kicks it."

"Good idea." I wink.

Jason glances both ways, as though he's about to cross a street, then pads to the table, leans down, and kisses me. "I'll dream about you, Lenny. Every night."

I'm fingering a nipple on his small, pumped chest when Edsel walks into the kitchen. I drop my hand, and Jason backs away.

"Why don't you fuck him right here on the table for everyone to watch!" Edsel screams. "I'm sure you've done as much to innocent boys before! I know your type!"

Purple-faced, Edsel stomps into the living room and out the front door.

"It's not like he *owns* me," Jason says, blushing and frowning. He shuts himself in the bathroom.

I hear a car start in front of the house and roll off the gravel.

Listening to the shower run, I finish my eggs and muffin, and carry my dishes to the sink.

Cleve zips his duffel bag, his back to me, as I pad into our room. He stiffens when the hears me creak the floorboards.

"I'm leaving. If you want to ride back with me, get your things together."

He hustles past me and walks to the rear of the house.

I put on my socks and shoes, stuff my damp swimsuit into my backpack, pull out my toothbrush, and brush my teeth with saliva and whatever paste is caked in the bristles.

Cleve comes back into the room, picks up his bag, and walks out the front door.

I crunch across the gravel behind him. He tosses his bag in the back seat, gets behind the wheel, and starts the engine. He unlocks my door. I get in and tuck my book bag at my feet.

We drive without talking. Cleve doesn't take curves fast, like some guys pissed off might. I glance over at him a couple of times.

The sun shines through tall evergreens and casts pools of light on car-sized boulders scattered among the trees. I want to get out, climb up on a rock, and join the lizards sunning themselves.

We catch up with a stream of cars coasting and braking down the mountain. Cleve has the air conditioner on, but I open my window partway because I'm cutting smelly farts.

"There's always a line of traffic in Southern California, wherever you go, whenever," I mumble.

We round another downhill curve.

"Sorry if I let you down this weekend, Cleve."

"I don't want your apology. I don't want anything from you."

"I guess I have that coming. What happened wasn't personal. I like to dick around, that's all. Dave's the only man who's ever been able to keep me on the porch."

"That's a hell of a reason to stay with someone."

I think about this as we round the next curve. It's a sensible reason, I decide.

"I never said I wasn't in love with Dave."

"Let's just ride and not talk."

Cleve stops at a Shell station in San Bernardino. When I offer him money while he pumps gas, he ignores me. I point at the john with my thumb. "I need to take a dump, okay?"

He doesn't answer.

Sitting on the toilet, I wonder if he'll be gone when I come out.

I open the john door and don't see Cleve's car by the gas pump. I hope it's parked along the other side of the building, but it isn't. I buy a Pepsi from a vending machine and sit on the blacktop with my legs folded, drinking and thinking how I brought this on myself. Then I realize my wallet is in my backpack in Cleve's car, and I just spent the money in my pocket on the Pepsi.

A couple in a sedan with an empty back seat are at a gas pump. I ask if they happen to be going to Orange County, and they look at me like I'm an escaped convict and shake their heads. Feeling foolish, I sit back down and lean against the building and wonder if I should ask someone to let me call Dave instead of trying for a ride.

Two men pull up to a pump in an SUV with a Cal State Fullerton decal. When I ask for a lift if they're going anywhere near Fullerton, they look at each other. The older one says okay.

We talk a little about CSF baseball as we drive, and then they talk between themselves about boats that the older one—the father—might buy. I think about the apology I plan to write Edsel. I'll write Don one, too. And send Cleve a book. I just have to figure out what book. He'll probably throw it away, whatever it is. He must really be hurting to leave me stranded.

I hate to have things end this way, hate myself for asking to go to Big Bear with him.

The SUV drops me at the bookstore, where my car is parked.

Dave leans against the kitchen counter at home, barefoot and shirtless in painter's pants, folded arms framing his large nipples. He stares at me as I look through the doorway from the living room. "How was Big Bear?"

"Nothing special."

The teakettle whistles, and he turns to the stove. A jar of instant coffee and his Georgetown mug sit on the counter.

As I strip the sheets off the open sofa bed in the den, I find my missing phone in the covers. I fold the bed into a couch, carry the dirty sheets into our bedroom, strip our double bed, put clean sheets on it, and bring the heap of laundry sheets to the kitchen.

Dave stands where he was, leaning against the counter and sipping from his mug. I smell his coffee as I stuff the bedding into the washer and start it. While the vibrating machine fills, I lean against it. "I need to take a shower. Maybe we could mess around when I get out? I put clean sheets on the bed."

"All right. Cleve dropped off your book bag. Said he went back but couldn't find you."

"I got a ride."

"He said he didn't tell you I returned your call yesterday. Apparently, you were in the shower. I said to tell you Stevie Wonder called. I wanted you to know I didn't forget our anniversary."

"I didn't forget either. That's why I called."

"We missed the day, but we don't have to miss the dance."

He holds his arms as though they have a dance partner in them and looks at me invitingly. I step into his embrace, and we waltz around our kitchen while Dave sings "I Just Called to Say I Love You." He knows all the words and has a good singing voice. He sang in his church choir during high school, even soloed some. In the past I've teased him about how rough high school must have been for him, being tall, good-looking, athletic, and a singer to boot. I've sometimes worried he'll wake up one day and decide he can do better than a guy who was a scrawny kid who couldn't catch or throw a baseball and didn't start muscling up until college.

"I'm sorry I've been such a shit to you lately," I say after our dance. "When I get out of the shower, I'll try to make it up to you."

Toweling off, I go damp to our bed, where Dave lies on his back. I kneel in the middle of the mattress and kiss his balls. First, I just plant my lips on them gently. Then I take one after the other in my mouth, moving back and forth, ball to ball, while I stretch my arms up to finger his nipples. His chest swells like a raging bull's. I tell him to show me his muscles, and he bends his arms. I could live the rest of my life with one of his balls in my mouth, his nipples at my fingertips, his biceps on display for me. I make him moan and squirm and flex like a god. When he can't hold it any longer, he spurts a fountain of white cream and gasps like a marathon runner at the finish line. I didn't touch his cock. Once before, I made him come by his balls and nipples and the sheer narcissism of showing off his muscles, and he said it was the most intense orgasm of his life. I hope this time was as good.

When he takes hold of my erection, I tell him I want to wait until later. We doze for a while. When we wake up, I raise my legs for him. That's when I come, while Dave makes my ass his again.

We heat up soup for a late lunch and eat at our dining table. Dave picks up his phone, fiddles with it, and hands it to me. I see a video of myself fucking, filmed from the foot of our bed. My feet, my legs, my butt, my back, just as I remember thinking in chorus as Dave filmed me fucking Ian. The back of my head shows. You can't see Ian beneath me. You can tell I'm fucking someone.

"You're so sexy, Len," Dave says. "Sex is to you like water is to an Olympic swimmer. It's the medium of your athleticism. I love that about you."

❖

Before I leave the bookstore on Monday, I stop next to Ian on his stool behind the register. "Can I come over when you get off work tonight?" I need to tell him I can't go to Baltimore. We have to be alone when I do it.

"Sure," he says.

At home, cleaning up after supper, I tell Dave I have to go out. "Cleve called, upset. I agreed to have a drink with him."

"*Why?*"

"He deserves more of an explanation than I gave him."

"He knew you had a husband."

I'm surprised by Dave's use of the word. Despite our rings, we never talk about ourselves as husbands. We haven't made it legal. We've said we're saving for a wedding, but I wonder if really we're saving marriage for a time when we aren't afraid one or both of us will succumb to a come-hither look from some cocksmith on the prowl. Marriage will be our wild card that wipes the slate clean, but it can only be played once.

"I didn't mean to hurt Cleve," I say to Dave. "He's a nice guy."

"You know him, I don't." After a shrug, Dave sighs and walks out of the kitchen.

When I'm ready to leave, I go to Dave's den and kiss him. I kiss him a second time and a third. After the fourth kiss, he relents. "Go talk to the guy. I'll be okay."

❖

On Ian's narrow mattress, with him lying spent on my chest, I whisper, "I have a question for you. Have you ever thought of going to UC Irvine instead of Hopkins?"

"Not recently."

"We could stay here."

"You don't want to leave Dave."

"I want you to move in with us."

He lifts off me and stands beside the bed. I touch his stomach with my fingertips, and he knocks my hand away.

"A few weeks ago you wanted Dave to go to Baltimore with you," I say.

"Where'd you get that idea?"

"It's true."

"It's not!"

"I saw a printout of Baltimore job ads on Dave's desk."

"He never said anything to me! I never said anything to him! You're the one who said you wanted to go away and start a life together. You said it didn't matter a *fuck* about Dave if I was in love with you."

Ian grabs white sweatpants off the floor, jabs his legs into them, and hustles out of the bedroom. I hop up and follow. He stands at the kitchen sink staring at the leggy branches of his backyard poinsettia tree in the light of suburban nighttime.

"Ian, I'm still in love with you. That's why I want you to move in with us."

"*Fuck.*"

"Dave's in love with you, too. He was thinking of going to Baltimore with you, whether he told you or not."

"I'm in love with *you*, Lenny." His voice breaks, he fights back tears. I try to put my arms around him, but he shoves me away. "Get out of my house and leave me alone!"

I grab him and pull him against me. "It doesn't have to be you-and-me, or me-and-Dave, or Dave-and-you. It can be all three of us." I kiss his salty cheeks, nuzzle his runny nose. When my erection burrows into the soft cloth of his sweatpants, he shoves me backward so hard I nearly trip.

"Get dressed and get out!" he bellows. "I mean it!"

"*Ian*, take it easy."

"Take it easy yourself! Get out!"

I walk into his bedroom, step into my underpants and jeans, and pull on my Haverford sweatshirt. He sits at the kitchen bar when I walk back into the living room. I stop by the front door, drop the flip-flops I carry, and toe into them.

"Think about it, Ian. I'm as much in love with you as I am with Dave."

I'm *not*, I realize. Not as much. "I'm as in love as a man can be." That's true. "Dave's in love with you." Infatuated, at least. "You'd be in love with him if you let yourself, Ian. No one has to choose."

He stares at the blank TV screen across the room while I let myself out.

❖

In the bookstore, Ian looks up from a paperback open on his lap. I stand by his stool at the register and wait for him to stop pretending he doesn't see me. I've stayed away from him for a couple of days.

"Have you thought about what I said, Ian?"

"Dave doesn't know about your plan, does he?"

"What do you expect? You've hardly seen Dave the past few weeks."

"You're so full of shit, Lenny."

"Come over tonight."

He raises his book between our faces.

Walking to my car, I check my cell for messages and find one telling me my flight to Baltimore will leave a half hour earlier. I cancel the ticket.

Dave's making skillet stroganoff at home. He's quiet, thinking about work, I assume. I wash my hands at the sink and take lettuce and tomatoes out of the refrigerator. He looks at me while he stirs ground beef, browning in a skillet. "There's an email message you need to look at, Len. I left it open on my computer."

On the email account we use when we buy things, I read the same message the airline sent to my phone. I take off my shoes and socks, toss them into our bedroom, and return to the kitchen. "I canceled that ticket," I tell Dave. "You're not going to Baltimore, and neither am I. We both had fantasies. Stir the ground beef—it's sticking."

❖

We spend a lazy Saturday entirely together. By late evening, we lounge in front of the TV. I curl on the guest room sofa in shorts and a T-shirt, Dave sits on the floor in jogging trunks and a tank shirt. I massage his neck and shoulders. A bottle of wine opened with dinner stands on the floor.

During a commercial, I go to piss. I hear our doorbell. Dave comes out of the guest room, and I zip up and follow him to the front of the house. Ian stands on our small cement porch. He wears a tight, white T-shirt, jeans, and flip-flips. "Lenny said I should drop by sometime." He eyes Dave.

"Good to see you," Dave says. Ian steps inside. His moist hair smells lemony. "We're watching a mystery we missed the beginning of. I'll open more wine." Dave heads into the kitchen.

I lead Ian into the guest room. He sits at one end of the sofa. I sit next to him.

Commercials flash in front of us. Dave brings a glass of wine for Ian and sets the newly opened bottle on a wood TV tray end table. He settles on the floor, near my feet, on my other side from Ian. The movie comes back on. I stroke Dave's ear, and he tilts his head toward my knee. I slip my other hand along the inseam of Ian's jeans. I feel his erection under the denim with my knuckles. I glance at his profile, his eyes fixed on the TV. I unsnap and unzip his jeans, push down the waistband of his underpants till his dick pops out. Gently I maneuver out his balls and finger them while the TV lights up his face.

Dave glances up, over his shoulder, and then looks back at the TV screen.

I scoot forward on the couch cushion, raise and splay my legs, wrap my thighs around Dave's broad neck. I unwrap my legs. Dave glances up again, and I hold Ian's bone away from his belly, displaying it. Then I peel off Dave's tank shirt. "Stand up, cowboy. Ian wants to suck your cock." Dave hesitates. I strip off Ian's T-shirt, and Dave rises to his feet. I push down Ian's jeans until they're around his ankles, like a tether. Dave removes his trunks. I use Dave's cock as a handle to position him in front of Ian, but not close enough for Ian to take Dave in his mouth. I let go of Dave's cock and force Ian's wrists together, against his stomach, as though he's handcuffed. I press him to the couch seat. "Look at that bead of pre-cum, Ian," I say, as Dave slowly moves his cock closer to Ian's mouth. Ian thrusts his head forward, but I keep his body pinned to the couch. Dave slowly brings his cock and its glistening pearl precisely to the tip of Ian's outstretched tongue.

❖

We spend the night on our queen-sized sofa bed. Ian lets both of us fuck him. He wants Dave's bigger body more than he wants mine, but he won't admit it even to himself. I don't care, as long as he's in our bed again.

8. HAVING IT ALL

Jane, at her desk across from me, smiles and talks on the phone, describing the pink suit she's wearing. With a plastic fork, she breaks off a tiny bite from a slice of yellow cake she's nibbled all afternoon. Driving to work, I stopped at a bakery in the small heart of town and picked up the cake with "Welcome back, Jane" written on top. Mai-Ly and Honey were at the bookstore when I got here. Rosie and Ian weren't scheduled but came in just after we opened, to be here when Jane arrived. At noon Jane hadn't arrived or called, and Rosie and Ian left. When I got back from the gym, Jane was at her desk. Honey and I stood by the counter while Mai-Ly brought the cake from the stockroom, and the three of us stepped into the office and said, "Welcome back, Jane."

"How sweet!" She clapped her hands together and nearly cried.

I felt like a schoolboy who normally gets into trouble on his best behavior. Mai-Ly and Honey served the cake, like PTA room mothers or the well-behaved girls in class. I handed Jane our welcome back card. "Rosie and Ian came in this morning, to be here for the occasion, but they couldn't stay," I said.

"Oh, I should have told you I had a doctor's appointment. We'll save some cake for them."

During the three hours since our little party, Jane's been on the phone.

Sitting at my desk, I glance out across the store to the parking lot, smoggier than it's been since fall and busier than usual. A couple of college-age Asian boys in shorts and flip-flops hop out of an old pickup with its windows down and pull on shirts. As I watch them disappear into an auto supply store next to the doughnut shop, I wonder if Jane really had a doctor's appointment, this being Memorial Day.

Rosie struggles through the front door with her purse and a book bag while she sips through a straw from a large paper cup. She's working for Ian this evening. He and Melinda are going to a beach party arranged by some lit department students. On Rosie's heels is a sunny-haired kid I recognize. I step out to the counter and lean across it. "Jeff."

"Jason," he says, laughing like I told a joke.

"Jason. Sorry. Jeff's the son of a friend of ours, another kid who laughs a lot. So what brings you to Royal Books?"

"I don't know," he says.

I straighten up from my lounging posture. My nose was too close to Jason's compact, pumped pecs in a loose red tank shirt that covers only one nipple or the other. Below his tank shirt are dark blue shorts with a swath of red at the thighs. Jason's biceps bulge even with his arms dangling. His calves bulge, too.

"You have an aunt in Brea, don't you?"

"La Habra."

"So you're visiting her?"

"Not really." Jason turns his head and glances around. I follow his eyes as they scan the store.

"Are you looking for something in particular?"

He shakes his head. His bright blue irises stare at me from a faintly tan face with cheeks as silky as a baby's.

Rosie, taking over the register from Mai-Ly, pretends she doesn't notice me talking to Jason. She'll tease me about him later.

"So you're not going to see your aunt?"

"Nah, I needed a break from lying around my room reading."

"For a break you drove all the way from...Malibu?"

"Oxnard. Well, to see you."

He laughs, and I laugh.

"Damn, Jason. I can't really spend much time visiting. I have to finish up a few things in my office and go home."

He bites his lip. I scratch my head. Suddenly my hair feels so thin, compared to the thick blond wave falling over his forehead.

"I had to see you, man." He stares at me like a scolded pup waiting for a sign of forgiveness. I glance over my shoulder at Jane in our office with the phone receiver cradled against her shoulder.

"Wait here a minute," I tell him.

At my desk, I pick up my phone and dial Dave. Jane will listen to every word I say even though she's in her own conversation. Dave answers.

"How would you feel about a dinner guest?" I ask.

"Fine, I suppose. Who?"

"A kid who came into the bookstore. He goes to Pepperdine. I know his folks in Texas." My lie is for Jane's ears. "They told him to look me up."

"I'll start the grill. I'm washing my car."

At the counter, I tell Jason my other half says to bring him home for dinner. "Do you have time before you drive back?"

"I guess so," he says, uncertainly.

"Go look at books while I do a couple of things, and then we'll leave."

I watch him wander into the science fiction aisle, his black strap sandals squeaking. Jane's still on the phone. I call our bookkeeper and leave a message with her husband, call a publisher's rep and leave a message on her phone, then try to catch Jane's eye as she stares at her blotter and gabs.

"No, dear, I was here in the store when it happened, sitting at my desk minding my own business...Exactly, yes! If I'd been home alone, who knows what might have happened."

On my feet, I wait for Jane to notice I'm standing by the door.

She looks up, and I nod to the front of the store. She smiles and wiggles two fingers, her way of waving when she's being the Good Little Girl. After a day or two more of the Good Little Girl, I'll welcome back the Bitch.

I collect Jason in the science fiction aisle. He's quiet as we walk outdoors. I tell him I'll bring him back to his car after dinner. I ask if he knew I was in a relationship.

"Yeah." He laughs.

"Not with Cleve."

"I know. Did you tell him we slept together?"

"He'll figure it out. You're way too cute."

"Will he kill me or anything?"

"Three other guys I slept with are buried in our backyard."

I wait for him to stop laughing.

"So who told you about Dave? Did I tell you?"

"Edsel told me. After you left, he warned me about guys like you. He said you're a chicken hawk."

I'm glad Jason finds this hilarious. While he busts a gut, I ease into a left turn pocket at a red light. We're on Valencia Drive, near home. A ranch-style firehouse sits on the corner, and I watch firemen washing their truck, one shirtless. He sees me looking at him, and I glance up at the stoplight just visible with the sun in my eyes.

"If I'm a chicken hawk, did Edsel say what he is?" I ask Jason. "Why do you hang around with Edsel anyhow?"

"He's fun, most of the time."

I catch myself about to say, "Shit, if you want fun, I can show your ass fun." The light switches to green, I roll into the intersection and turn after a few cars pass. I ask Jason why he goes to Pepperdine.

"My dad teaches in the music department. I get tuition reimbursement."

"Do you like it?"

"It's all right."

"It's a Christian college, isn't it?"

"Afraid so."

"You're not religious?"

"Not the way some people are."

I slow down and park in front of our house.

"Dave went to Wheaton. He says he wasn't religious by the time he got there. His folks are Christian with a capital C, his mom at least."

We climb out of my car. I lead Jason up the walk, unlock the front door, and grab the mail, which I drop on the kitchen counter before pulling two bottles of beer from the refrigerator and handing one to Jason. He follows me out back. Dave, in dark blue jogging shorts, is tugging the hose in from the alley, his pale chest and limbs glistening with sun block. "You guys are earlier than I expected. I'll get the charcoal lit."

"No hurry. This is Jason. Jason, this is Dave."

They shake hands. I smile watching Jason try not to ogle Dave's body and watching Dave enjoy Jason's struggle. I unknot my tie and pull it free from my shirt collar. "While you guys get to know each other, I'll change clothes. By the way,

Dave, I only said I know Jason's parents because I didn't want Jane snooping in my business. Jason was up at Big Bear."

I head up the walk to the house.

Folding my trousers over a hanger in our bedroom, I stare at a pair of Ian's jeans in the closet next to a couple of his shirts. Most of Ian's clothes are in our guest room, where he and Dave and I have slept on the sofa bed for the past nine nights. We ordered a king-sized bed that will fill our bedroom when it's delivered. Ian still goes home every day, usually showers at home or at the college gym. But in a few weeks, ours will be the only home he has to go to.

I wonder how late he'll be out with Melinda tonight.

In shorts without underwear and a ragged Hawaiian shirt that I leave unbuttoned, I head to the kitchen and begin mashing ground beef into patties. Through the screen door, I watch Dave and Jason stand by our grill. Jason's tank shirt is off, wadded in one fist. He and Dave are talking and laughing, while flames dance in bright daylight above the grill's surface. A plume of white smoke drifts off. I catch the word "Wheaton" in Dave's hale voice.

After washing raw beef off my hands, I carry a platter of six patties outside. Our jade tree hedge is in deep shade along the block wall, our red bougainvillea in full sun and full bloom against the garage. Dave smiles at Jason, who laughs and says, "No shit." Jason sees me and blushes. I reach up and ruffle his hair.

"Getting a few rays and checking out each other's beefcake, huh, guys?"

Jason laughs and blushes deeper.

A rusty TV tray leans against the block wall. One-handed, I fumble open the tray and slide the platter of hamburger patties on it. Dave and Jason watch without offering to help, brain dead from all the blood rushing to their dicks, I figure. Laughing at Dave, I ease a fingertip into his navel.

"What?" he says, acting innocent, while my finger plays umbilical cord.

"Nothing, cowboy."

"Do you need help inside?"

"No, entertain our guest and grill the hamburgers."

I tweak Jason's nipple and pad up the narrow walk.

I'm slicing an onion, wiping tears with the back of my hand, when Jason comes looking for the bathroom. I smile and point the knife through the living room.

Dave comes in, takes a spatula out of a drawer, and nods at the sound of Jason's stream hitting toilet water. "How well do you know him, anyhow?"

"How well do you think?"

Dave leans back laughing. "Is that what happened between you and Cleve up at Big Bear?"

I shrug, and Dave laughs harder.

"Like I told Cleve, you're the only man who can keep me on the porch."

Dave kisses my cheek, and I squeeze his half-boner through his jogging shorts.

"Getting a hard-on for Jason, cowboy?"

"Fuck, he's cute enough. Jesus."

The toilet flushes, and Dave heads out the back door with his spatula. Jason's black strap sandals squish on their soles as he comes into the kitchen.

"You're welcome to another beer, Jason, but remember you'll be driving later."

"Maybe a Coke?"

I hand him a can from the refrigerator.

"Dave's a nice guy."

"He is. And a hunk, huh?"

Jason laughs like I told my most entertaining joke of all time. I grin and slice a tomato in half.

"Do me a favor, Jas. Grab a chair from the dining table and set it on the patio with the two webbed chairs."

Jason steps into the front room and returns carrying a dining chair. I prop open the screen door with my toes while he backs outside.

Sitting on the patio we eat hamburgers and cantaloupe and talk about college.

Jason stands by my shoulder while I load our dirty plates in the dishwasher. When I turn around, Dave leans against the washing machine, hands locked behind his neck, arms raised like wings, showing lots of silky brown armpit hair and muscle. Jason stares at Dave and shoves his hands deep in the pockets of his shorts. Dave's nostrils flare with the deep breathing that expands and contracts his chest.

I move behind Jason, wrap my arms around his small pumped torso, and find his nipples with my thumbs. Dave lowers an arm and runs a hand over his own pecs and down to his navel. Watching us watch him, he slowly lowers the waistband of his jogging trunks along the length of his erection until it bobs free. He steps closer to Jason, who takes hold of it.

"Why don't we move into the bedroom," I say quietly.

Kneeling on the side of our high double bed, I watch Dave edge his cock between Jason's buttocks while Jason grits his teeth, his knuckles clamped like vise grips on the pencil eraser–sized nubs of Dave's nipples. "I'll stop whenever you tell me to," Dave says. "Take a deep breath."

Through the corner of my eye, I glimpse Ian in the doorway. He's gone by the time I turn my head.

Dave starts to rock, out and in, while Jason gulps air.

I back off the bed and pull on my shorts. Dave stops moving and looks over at me.

"Ian's home," I say quietly. "Go on. I'll be right back."

Dave looks down at Jason, hesitates, and slowly moves his hips forward. I close the door as I leave.

Ian sits in the center of our living room couch, elbows on his knees. He stares at the dark wood floor. I sit beside him and lay my hand on his shoulder. He straightens with a jerk and bats my arm away.

"Come on, Ian. He's just some kid I met. I brought him home for dinner, and one thing led—"

"I'd expect it of *you*."

"Dave's human—you proved that."

Ian stands up.

"What are you doing home?" I ask. "I thought you were going to the beach."

"I came to get a jacket." He walks slowly to the front door and out. I watch through our picture window as he climbs into his car and drives off.

Our box spring creaks rhythmically in the other room. The refrigerator motor comes on and nearly drowns out the sound.

I make a pot of coffee and carry a mug to the couch. I sip, staring at the artificial log in the unignited fireplace. A greeting card with Renoir's *Boating Party* on front stands on the mantel. Dave gave it to me on my birthday the first year we were together. He bought it at the Phillips Collection, near our Washington apartment. I found it in a drawer the other day and got it out.

I pour another mug of coffee and return to the couch. The box spring, after being silent awhile, begins to creak again.

It's dusk when our bedroom door opens, and Dave goes across the hall floor to the bathroom. The streetlamp in front of our house comes on and shines through the picture window at my back. Jason steps out in the hall, his plump dick floppy. I smile, and he laughs. He looks out the window and holds a hand over his genitals. "I left my trunks in the kitchen."

"No one can see. The cars go by too fast."

I follow Jason into the kitchen and grin watching him stumble into his underpants and shorts. "Dave fucked you good? You fucked him, too, huh? You had your dick in my cowboy," I say in a tone of mock scolding.

He grins. "I never did that before, either way."

Dave comes into the kitchen in his jogging shorts, his brown hair falling over one eye, his nipples as red as rouge. He looks at me sheepishly, like he thinks I might be mad. I peck him on the lips and press my fingers to his ribs. "Sore tits, cowboy?"

He smiles and gives me a real kiss. "Where's Ian?"

"He just dropped by to get a jacket." I turn to Jason and ask if he'd like a cup of coffee.

"How late is it?"

I glance at the stove clock. "Five past eight."

"I should go soon."

"Have a cup of coffee for the road." I fill a mug for him, take the milk carton out of the refrigerator and the sugar bowl from a cabinet. "Do you want to jump in the shower, Jas?"

"Could I?"

"Sure. Take your coffee. I'll get you a towel."

I fetch one from the linen closet and hand it to him. He shrugs off his shorts and underpants. I snap a mental picture of his sated dick curved over his testicles, and then wink and leave him alone.

Dave gulps apple juice as he leans against the stove. He lowers the glass. "Why didn't you come back to bed, Len?"

"I didn't need to."

"You're not upset with me?"

"Not at all." I kiss him.

"What'd Ian say?"

"He said, 'I'd expect it of *you*'—meaning me."

"Shit. I feel bad."

"He'll get over it."

The shower cuts off.

"That was quick," I mumble.

Still frowning, Dave raises his plastic tumbler and gulps. I pull the basket out of the coffeemaker and run the soggy grounds down the disposal.

Jason looks more wet than dry as he pads into the kitchen in his tank shirt and trunks.

"Fast shower," I say.

"I didn't know where to put the towel so I hung it over the rod?"

"That's fine."

He sets his empty mug in the sink, picks up his black sandals from the floor, and stands on one foot, then the other, strapping them on. "I really should be going. You know, living with my parents."

"Sure, we understand," I say.

"Thanks for dinner."

"Thanks for *dinner*?" I grin at Dave. "The guy fucks his brains out, and all he thanks us for is dinner?"

"Thanks for that, too."

"I'm teasing you, Jason. You don't have to thank anyone for a fuck. No one does. But especially hot stuff like you doesn't. Come on, I'll drive you back to your car."

"Maybe I'll jump in the shower while Lenny gives you a ride?" Dave says.

I nod. Dave walks with us to the door, gives Jason a kiss. "If you ever want to talk or anything, just call or come by," Dave says. "Understand?"

Looking embarrassed, Jason nods.

"I'll be right back, cowboy. Get in the shower."

Jason's quiet as we drive toward the bookstore. He laughs when I squeeze his leg and tell him to remember about condoms. "Don't let a few beers make you careless."

"I'm not stupid."

"I know you're not."

He directs me to his car, a hatchback like mine, only white, parked in the empty center of the lot. "Thanks again, man. For everything."

"Sure, Jas. Our pleasure."

I smile while he laughs. He gets out of my car and into his. Glancing inside the bookstore, I see a woman standing by the greeting cards and see Rosie and Honey talking behind the counter. Jason's car starts, and I follow it from the parking lot. He goes to the freeway. I turn at the corner.

On Orangethorpe Avenue, I drive past our street, by the Methodist church that reminds me of Michael, then turn to cross over the freeway, and turn again into Ian's neighborhood. His house, third from the corner, is dark, and his car isn't in the driveway. I wait with my engine idling, staring at the black windows, thinking Ian might drive up. I wonder if his car could be in the garage, although I know he always parks in the driveway. I phone and leave a message. "Call so I know you're all right." I text him the same message.

I head home, hoping he'll be at our house. When he isn't, I figure he's at Melinda's.

Dave and I tuck in for the night on our sofa bed. Wide awake from drinking too much coffee, I listen to traffic pass on Brookhurst while I worry about Ian. I try to remember if I've ever been inside his garage. I haven't. Probably nothing is in it, because he cleared it out to sell the house.

At three in the morning I sit on the couch in our shadowy living room trying to recall exactly what I saw when I waited in my car, idling in front of Ian's house. I remember the streetlamp shining on his crabgrass lawn and on the dark living room window and on the freshly painted front door. My mind's eye moves along the beige stucco exterior of the house to the attached garage. Did I see exhaust rising from the vent just above ground level in Ian's garage?

Ian is close to Melinda, if to no one else except Dave and me. He knows we all care about him.

During the year Dave and I lived apart in Washington, I shared a two-bedroom apartment with a manic-depressive straight guy named Hayden. I try not to think about the premonition I had as I walked from the kitchen to Hayden's room. I told myself I was being ridiculous to feel concerned over the fact that I hadn't seen Hayden all day. I knocked and, when he didn't answer, opened the door and found Hayden dead. He'd overdosed.

I know my experience with Hayden left me inclined to hysterical imaginings. I rise from the couch and return to our sofa bed. Daylight creeps into the room as I fall asleep, my foot touching Dave's for grounding. His steady breathing lulls me.

I wake to news on the clock radio and hit the snooze bar. I hit the snooze bar twice more. Dave isn't teaching today and sleeps on.

In the shower, with sun lighting up the window above the tub, I feel more levelheaded than I felt sitting on the couch in the middle of the night. After I dry off, I phone Ian and leave a message saying to call me.

Driving to work, I tell myself the queasiness in my stomach, the tingling in my limbs, is from lack of sleep.

I call Ian again in mid-morning. I call Dave and get his message center. I look up Melinda's number, dial, reach an anonymous answering system and leave no message.

My gym bag isn't in my car as I climb in at lunchtime. I forgot it when I left the house.

Empty garbage cans are tipped over along Valencia Drive, in front of pale two-story apartment buildings lined with palm trees and parked cars. Ahead of me, a motorcycle pulls out from the curb and crackles and backfires. As the motorcycle and I turn left at Brookhurst by the fire station, I know I'll pass home, drive on to Ian's house, and open the garage.

I'm so intent on getting to Ian's house that I drive by his old Ford parked in front of our place. Pulling to the curb, and then backing toward his car, I laugh out loud. I need sleep, I tell myself.

A rock tape blares in the living room. Noon light floods through the window, across the wood floor, and into the kitchen, shining on Dave's and Ian's bare backsides in front of the stove. They don't hear me walk up behind them. I pat both their butts, and they nearly jump out of their skins.

"What brings you home?" Dave asks, laughing.

"I forgot my gym clothes. What have you two been doing?"

They smile. I watch an omelet take shape in a small skillet as I slip an arm around Ian's waist. "Does this mean I'm out of the doghouse, too?"

Smirking, Ian shrugs. I move my mouth close to his, and he kisses me.

I see his phone lying on the counter. "Don't you listen to your messages or look at your texts? I was worried about you." I press another kiss on him.

"Sorry," he says and picks up his phone.

"Do you want an omelet?" Dave says.

"I was planning to go to the gym, although I feel more like a nap."

"Stay and have an omelet. One's done."

Dave shoves a spatula under the omelet in the skillet. Glasses of orange juice sit on the sink counter, the aroma of coffee wafts from the pot. Dave holds a chipped blue plate out for me. Staring at the omelet, I wonder how I feel about Dave and Ian going to bed, getting up, and cooking bare-assed. Dave will be working at home all summer. Ian will be home with him until five o'clock.

"No, I'm going to the gym," I say. "You guys enjoy lunch." I hand the plate to Ian.

I pick up my gym bag from the bedroom floor.

"See you later," I shout over the music as I pass through the living room. My car's warm from sitting in the sun, and the floor mat's sticky from a Dr Pepper I spilled yesterday. The air conditioner isn't working, so I open the windows.

I'm so tired at the gym, I just sit and pedal a stationary bicycle. I wonder how Tony is doing in Seattle.

❖

The lamp is on by the sofa bed because I want to see Ian's face contort when he comes. He's straddling my chest, his cock barely more than half-mast in my mouth—I suspect he and Dave went to bed again after their omelets. Ian looked super relaxed when he sauntered into the bookstore at five.

Dave, kneeling by my legs, leans behind Ian and takes my cock in his mouth. I'm about to feed Dave my load, when Ian suddenly rises on his upper legs and yanks away from me. I push up on my elbows, chasing his cock with my mouth.

"I can't do this, Lenny."

I look up into Ian's dark blue eyes. Dave lets me bob out of his mouth and straightens up on his knees.

Ian shakes his head. "Maybe I could be lovers with either of you, but I can't be lovers with both of you. I want it all. You guys have it all."

Ian climbs off my chest, off the bed. He stares at Dave and me as we stare at him. I sit up on the mattress, and Dave and I glance at each other. Dave's still kneeling, upper legs and spine straight, tall even on his knees. "You deserve it all, Ian," he says.

Ian looks at the floor, picks up his underwear and jeans, and kicks into them. He picks up a pale blue T-shirt and pulls it over his head.

Dave crawls off the bed. I turn sideways, put my feet to the floor, and watch Ian wiggle his toes around the thongs of his black flip-flops. He heads for the front of the house, and Dave and I follow.

"You don't have to leave," I call after him.

"I want to be alone."

"Are you okay?"

"I will be. I need time to think."

Dave and I watch him climb into his car and drive off.

I linger, naked, behind the open door while a handful of cars pass on Brookhurst. The midnight air feels good—our house hasn't cooled off from another warm day.

Once I close the door, I look at Dave, perched with one buttock on the couch arm. He takes my hand, leads me to the kitchen, and gets milk out of the refrigerator and Oreos out of a cabinet. Sitting at the dining table, we eat cookies and drink milk.

We floss and brush our teeth for a second time tonight. I open the window wider in our guest room.

"Let him sleep on it," Dave says as we settle on our sofa bed. He slides down and finishes off my cock.

❖

I watch from my desk as Ian walks through the bookstore's glass doors, the late afternoon sun blazing on the parking lot behind him. He wears a tan T-shirt and tan pants and looks well-scrubbed and impassive. He disappears into the stockroom, reappears, and walks behind the counter. I nod to him as his flip-flops slap past my office door.

While he takes over the register from Honey, our UPS man hands a small box to him. After Honey leaves, Ian brings the box to my door. "This came overnight delivery. Are you expecting it?"

"Jane is—earrings and a necklace for her daughter-in-law's birthday tomorrow."

I stand up and lean across my desk to set the small box on Jane's blotter. Ian waits while I call Jane's house and leave a message.

"I have a favor to ask, Lenny."

"Sure, anything."

"This is a big one. I want to quit Friday."

"Quit work? *Why?*"

"I'm going to Ireland. I got a seat on a flight to Dublin Saturday."

"What about your house?"

"The estate lawyer will handle settlement. I don't want to leave you in the lurch here. I called Rosie, and she wants most of my shifts since she's staying another month."

"You're certain you want to do this?"

He nods.

"What about school?"

"I'll get to Baltimore in time to find an apartment. I wonder if I could leave a few boxes for you guys to send when I have an address?"

"Sure. But, Ian, why run away?"

"I'm not running away. I'd planned to go to Ireland two summers ago. I had a plane ticket and my passport, but my mom wound up in the hospital. Last night, I realized I can go."

I stand up and put my arms around him, shut my eyes, hug him tight. "We're still friends, right?"

"Always, Lenny."

❖

At home I tell Dave the news.

"Makes sense," he says.

"I guess." I open the freezer to see what we can heat up for dinner. "At least I won't have to worry about you guys fixing omelets bare-assed without me."

"Were you going to worry about that?"

"A little," I admit, smiling.

❖

Dave and I and Ian and Melinda climb silently out of our car. Melinda balances a potted daisy on one hand and smooths her gray slacks with the other. Dave and I follow her and Ian on a lawn and between rows of graves with flat markers. She and Ian stop by a grave covered with newer grass than those around it. Dave and I hang back. Melinda bends over, brushes loose dirt off the marker with her hand, and sets the potted daisy on the grave.

Ian bows his head. When his shoulders quake, Melinda puts her arm around him.

He raises his head, and Melinda takes his hand. They turn our direction, and Ian stares at our car, his cheeks wet below his sunglasses. They start walking. Dave and I turn and lead the way.

Dave drives slowly along the road toward the exit.

"I think I'll stop buying clothes that wrinkle so easily," Melinda says as we turn out of the cemetery.

Dave glances in the rearview mirror. "Lenny and I don't even own an iron."

"Men are lucky. Ian can pack two tote bags for the whole summer. Ian, did you tell the guys about Robert and Lila's offer?"

"Robert and Lila invited me to stay with them during their six weeks in London."

I glance over the seat back. "Great."

"In Dublin, I'm staying with a woman my mom worked for and lived with. She's all excited I'm coming. I don't know how much of her mothering I'll be able to take. I haven't seen her since she came here when I was ten."

"Mrs. O.," I say. I remember him mentioning her not long after his mother's funeral.

"Mrs. O. She told me my father's last name is Costello, and that Costellos are black Irish, supposedly descendants of shipwrecked sailors from the Spanish Armada. My father was a grocer's son. His father forbade him to marry my mom. They were seventeen when she got pregnant."

I do a quick calculation. "Your mom was only forty-three when she died?"

"She lived a short, not-so-happy life. I always thought I should have been enough to make her happy."

I think about this as we drive down a slope on wide Brea Boulevard, between condo developments in folds of brown foothills.

"I don't know, Ian. I love my mom and enjoy her company, but she wouldn't be enough to make me happy."

"Exactly," Melinda says.

I look over the seat back, and Ian nods.

In the glare of smoggy sunshine, we ride through Fullerton's small downtown, with its median of floss silk trees. We roll by a vintage clothing place and then by the furniture store where Dave and I canceled our order for a new bed. We roll down the vine-covered underpass beneath the railroad tracks.

As we approach Royal Books, in front of its nameless strip mall, I stare at the store's beige side and back walls, all that's visible from Harbor Boulevard—an architectural blunder for a retail business, a blunder I'm probably more conscious of because I've decided to go to architecture school. I'll work part-time somewhere other than Royal Books while I'm studying.

Ian's flight is scheduled to leave from the international terminal. In the unloading zone, I jump out and hold the car door open. Ian and Melinda hug in the back seat. Dave gets Ian's duffel bags out, and he and Ian hug. Ian turns to me. "I guess this is it," he says.

I crumple into tears in his arms.

"Friends always, Lenny," he says softly, letting me go.

I nod and suck back mucus, feeling foolish. He picks up his bags and disappears through the glass doors.

Melinda is the first to speak on the drive home.

"Isn't it nice that we don't have to worry about Ian being alone? He'll be with his mother's friend in Dublin, and with Robert and Lila in London. We can all go see him in Baltimore."

"We should," Dave says.

I'm too embarrassed about having cried to do more than

nod. Melinda and Dave talk about teaching. My mind moves ahead to something I want to do when Dave and I get home.

At Melinda's apartment complex, near the college, I give her a helping hand as she climbs out of our back seat.

"We're having a barbecue next Saturday," I mumble. "Robert and Lila will be there, Sandy and her son, Jeff—he's coming home for summer. I don't know whether you've met Jeff?"

"I've heard her talk about him."

"Maybe some other people you know. Not a big crowd. You're invited, if you're free."

"Yummy. What can I bring?"

"Just yourself. We're telling people five o'clock, right, Dave?"

"Five o' clock. Later's fine, or earlier."

"I should jot down our address for you."

"I know where you live. See you next Saturday."

She gives me a light hug and follows a short walkway to exterior stairs to the balcony corridor of a sand-colored building.

As Dave and I drive home, I tell him what I'd like to do when we get there.

Coming out of the bedroom, after taking off my shirt and shoes, I see Dave's big white naked body standing on our walled lawn with his back to me. Our soaker hose wafts a fine mist over a small wrestling mat Dave dragged across country as a pad for moving the headboard and footboard of his grandparents' double bed. I take off my pants and join him outside. We spend the afternoon making love in the sunlit spray of our hose while our own private rainbow arcs over us.

About the Author

Gary Garth McCann's fiction includes the gay novella *Young and in Love?* and the noir legal thriller *The Man Who Asked to Be Killed*, along with stories in *Chelsea Station Magazine*, *Erotic Review Magazine*, *Mobius: A Journal of Social Change*, *Off the Rocks*, *Best Gay Love Stories 2005*, and the *Harrington Gay Men's Fiction Quarterly*. He's been honored by Maryland Writers' Association first prizes for short fiction and mystery. He married Todd Garth, the US Naval Academy's first out professor, on their 25th anniversary and uses Todd's surname as a middle name for writing.

Visit Gary's blog at garygarthmccann.com. Contact him at garygarthmccann@gmail.com.

Books Available From Bold Strokes Books

The Shape of the Earth by Gary Garth McCann. After appearing in *Best Gay Love Stories*, *HarringtonGMFQ*, *Q Review*, and *Off the Rocks*, Lenny and his partner Dave return in a hotbed of manhood and jealousy. (978-1-63555-391-8)

Exit Plans for Teenage Freaks by 'Nathan Burgoine. Cole always has a plan—especially for escaping his small-town reputation as "that kid who was kidnapped when he was four"—but when he teleports to a museum, it's time to face facts: it's possible he's a total freak after all. (978-1-163555-098-6)

Death Checks In by David S. Pederson. Despite Heath's promises to Alan to not get involved, Heath can't resist investigating a shopkeeper's murder in Chicago, which dashes their plans for a romantic weekend getaway. (978-1-163555-329-1)

Of Echoes Born by 'Nathan Burgoine. A collection of queer fantasy short stories set in Canada from Lambda Literary Award finalist 'Nathan Burgoine. (978-1-63555-096-2)

The Lurid Sea by Tom Cardamone. Cursed to spend eternity on his knees, Nerites is having the time of his life. (978-1-62639-911-2)

Sinister Justice by Steve Pickens. When a vigilante targets citizens of Jake Finnigan's hometown, Jake and his partner Sam fall under suspicion themselves as they investigate the murders. (978-1-63555-094-8)

Club Arcana: Operation Janus by Jon Wilson. Wizards, demons, Elder Gods: Who knew the universe was so crowded, and that they'd all be out to get Angus McAslan? (978-1-62639-969-3)

Triad Soul by 'Nathan Burgoine. Luc, Anders, and Curtis—vampire, demon, and wizard—must use their powers of blood, soul, and magic to defeat a murderer determined to turn their city into a battlefield. (978-1-62639-863-4)

Gatecrasher by Stephen Graham King. Aided by a high-tech thief, the Maverick Heart crew race against time to prevent a cadre of savage corporate mercenaries from seizing control of a revolutionary wormhole technology. (978-1-62639-936-5)

Wicked Frat Boy Ways by Todd Gregory. Beta Kappa brothers Brandon Benson and Phil Connor play an increasingly dangerous game of love, seduction, and emotional manipulation. (978-1-62639-671-5)

Death Goes Overboard by David S. Pederson. Heath Barrington and Alan Keyes are two sides of a steamy love triangle as they encounter gangsters, con men, murder, and more aboard an old lake steamer. (978-1-62639-907-5)

A Careful Heart by Ralph Josiah Bardsley. Be careful what you wish for…love changes everything. (978-1-62639-887-0)

Worms of Sin by Lyle Blake Smythers. A haunted mental asylum turned drug treatment facility exposes supernatural detective Finn M'Coul to an outbreak of murderous insanity, a strange parasite, and ghosts that seek sex with the living. (978-1-62639-823-8)

Tartarus by Eric Andrews-Katz. When Echidna, Mother of all Monsters, escapes from Tartarus and into the modern world, only an Olympian has the power to oppose her. (978-1-62639-746-0)

Rank by Richard Compson Sater. Rank means nothing to the heart, but the Air Force isn't as impartial. Every airman learns that rank has its privileges. What about love? (978-1-62639-845-0)

The Grim Reaper's Calling Card by Donald Webb. When Katsuro Tanaka begins investigating the disappearance of a young nurse, he discovers more missing persons, and they all have one thing in common: The Grim Reaper Tarot Card. (978-1-62639-748-4)

Smoldering Desires by C.E. Knipes. Evan McGarrity has found the man of his dreams in Sebastian Tantalos. When an old boyfriend from Sebastian's past enters the picture, Evan must fight for the man he loves. (978-1-62639-714-9)

www.ingramcontent.com/pod-product-compliance
Lightning Source LLC
Chambersburg PA
CBHW030514020726
47494CB00004B/1090